The Mythopoeic Society

50

1967 · Fiftieth Anniversary · 2017

The Mythic Circle

#46: 2024

Victoria Gaydosik
Manager and Fiction Editor

Nolan Meditz
Poetry Editor

Phillip Fitzsimmons
Archivist and Proofreader

Information for Aspiring Contributors

The Mythic Circle solicits original unpublished fantasy-inspired stories and poems from the membership of the Mythopoeic Society and from the larger world—anyone may contribute, but we give first consideration to our membership. We are also looking for original visual art contributions in the form of jpeg or other suitable file formats. We publish an annual volume each midsummer in time for the Society's conference or online seminar; submissions are accepted year-round.

A small literary magazine, *The Mythic Circle* is published electronically and/or for print-on-demand by the **Mythopoeic Society**, an organization that celebrates the work of J. R. R. Tolkien, C. S. Lewis, Charles Williams, and the other Inklings. These innovative writers drew upon the rich tradition of imaginative speculative narratives and returned fantasy to a respectable place in serious literature, and we carry on in their tradition. An affordable annual membership in the Society is available at http://www.mythsoc.org/join.htm.

The editors look mostly for original work by authors following the mythic tradition; this *can* include a certain amount of commentary and allusion to the works of other mythic authors (though such allusions and commentary are not necessary). However, the editors do not wish to see "fan fiction" such as stories that make use of characters or settings from works by living or recent authors or artists or any works still under copyright.

Submissions and letters of comment should be e-mailed to mythiccircle@mythsoc.org. Contributors may also join (for free) the SWOSU Digital Commons, the archival repository of the Mythopoeic Society, and use the submission portal, located at the following URL: https://dc.swosu.edu/cgi/submit.cgi?context=mcircle. Joining the Digital Commons will also provide extensive statistical feedback to contributors about worldwide downloads.

Table of Contents

Our Contributors
#46: 2024

Hua Ai (Nikolina) is an educator based in London. She is a published feminist writer in Mandarin. Her English poetry engages with the spiritual animals in her mind palace, cultural feminism, and sisterhood. She is actively researching pragmatic approaches to promote animal rights. In the meantime, she is an experienced runner and occasionally retreats to the Baltic Sea.

L. C. Atencio was the illustrator for *The Mythic Circle* issues 34, 35, 36, 37 and 38. After *The Mythic Circle*, he expanded his professional career via exhibiting artworks in art festivals and working for other press houses.

Jared M. Bentley (he/him/his) is a humble mortal who lives happily with his partner in Ypsilanti, Michigan. Much of his time is spent grading student writing and coaching tennis. When he is not writing or working, he can often be found walking his dog, playing disc golf, or eating a sandwich.

Jacob Bier is a pastor and poet living in Pennsylvania who enjoys writing on theological and mythological themes. More of his writing can be found at bierjake.wordpress.com.

Kevan Kenneth Bowkett has been in the Canadian Reserves, washed dishes, planted trees, slept in an igloo, and run for Parliament. He's lectured at universities and worked in a daycare. His play *Time's Fancy: The War of King Henry V and Joan of Arc* was shown at the Winnipeg Fringe Theatre Festival in 2017. His work has appeared in *Mythprint*, the *Manitoba Eco-Journal*, and earlier editions of *The Mythic Circle*. His recent books (2020) include *The City of Sapphires* and *Seachild*, the latter set in the fabled land of Cothirya (on Amazon).

Lawrence Buentello is a writer and poet living in San Antonio, TX. A short-story specialist, he has published innumerable tales in the fantasy, horror, and science fiction genres. He holds a traditional degree in English literature and has twenty-five years of experience working in academic libraries.

Kenneth Burtness has been a member of Sammath Naur for 48 years. He has just finished a short book on the Tarot and the I Ching. He is currently working on three fantasy books: *8 Trees*, about prehistoric Hawaii; *Cantaloupe Genes*, a psychosexual look at reincarnation; and *Rox in a Box*, about the mind surviving the demise of the body. He has an M.A. in Social Psychology, and he is currently doing a local public awareness television show for ThinkTechHawaii called "Finding Happiness in Hard Times."

Christopher Collingwood was born and raised in Sydney Australia. He completed university in Sydney and graduated with a degree in business studies. Chris has devoted his spare time to writing, with works published in *Not One of Us*, *Andromeda Spaceways*, *Abyss & Apex*, *Hexagon*, *Shoreline of Infinity*, *Jersey Devil Press*, *State of Matter*, *Smoke in the Stars anthology*, *Qualia Nous*: Vol. 2 and illustrations in the recent *JOURN-E 2.1* and *The Sprawl Mag 2.1*, among other dimensionally unstable places.

Andoni Cossio is Assistant Professor of English at the University of the Basque Country (UPV/EHU). He is also Research Affiliate at the Centre for Fantasy and the Fantastic (University of Glasgow). His writing on C. S. Lewis, William Shakespeare, and mostly J. R. R. Tolkien has been published in: *ANQ*; *English Studies*; *The Explicator*; *ISLE*; *Multicultural Shakespeare*; *Journal of Inklings Studies*; *SELIM*; and in peer-reviewed edited collections of essays. In his free time, he indulges a growing passion for creative writing which often contains academic interpolations. ORCID: 0000-0003-2745-5104, ehu.academia.edu/AndoniCossio.

Holly Day currently teaches at the Loft Literary Center in Minnesota, the Richard Hugo House in Washington, and WriterHouse in Virginia, and her recent book publications include *Music Composition for*

Dummies, The Tooth is the Largest Organ in the Human Body, and *Bound in Ice.* She teaches creative writing at The Loft Literary Center in Minneapolis and Hugo House in Seattle.

David Ehrenman is a passionate supporter of mythopoeia, and had the privilege of earning Highest Distinction in his B.A. degree in English Literature with a concentration in Medieval and Renaissance Studies from the University of Virginia. He now channels his love for mythopoeic storytelling into creative writing.

Eleanor Farrell is a writer of eclectic travel and pop culture essays and Not-Ready-for-Mythcon plays who recently dipped her toes back into fiction and poetry. A longtime member of the Mythopoeic Society, she served as editor of *Mythprint* and as Mythopoeic Awards Administrator and created the group's first web site back in the dim times. Mostly retired from a parade of not very lucrative employments (teacher, graphic designer, jelly doughnut stuffer, molecular biology researcher), she enjoys most everything put in her path, from baseball and East Coast pizza to good booze and travel through time and space.

Phillip Fitzsimmons is the University Archivist & Special Collections Librarian at Southwestern Oklahoma State University (SWOSU) in Weatherford, Oklahoma, responsible for the General Thomas P. Stafford Archives. He is also the administrator of the SWOSU Digital Commons https://dc.swosu.edu/, and also manages the Mythopoeic Society's (Mythsoc) physical and digital collections as the Steward for Society Archives. The Mythsoc digital repository is found at https://dc.swosu.edu/mythsoc/. His research interests include digital services for academic libraries. He has also presented and published on the works of J.R.R. Tolkien, C.S. Lewis, Owen Barfield, and the Inklings. He began making stained glass over 20 years ago.

Jon Heggestad is a writer and an educator. His works have appeared in publications including *Public Books, The Lion & the Unicorn,* and *Transformative Works & Cultures.* He is also a contributor to *Xtra Magazine.*

S. R. Horgan has been published in *Verily* and *Ekstasis.* She lives in Texas with her husband and son.

Caroline Hunt is a sometime photographer and student of life living in Oklahoma.

Mary Johnson has loved stories since she knew they existed, and has written to entertain friends and family from age eight. Her father introduced her to C.S. Lewis and J.R.R. Tolkien; her mother, to the Greek myths. She worked as a librarian for 29 years and is now an aspiring novelist. Her poetry and short stories have appeared in *The Nonbinary Review, The Westchester Review,* online in *Sick Lit Magazine* and in issues 31 and 46 of *The Mythic Circle.* You can find her online at http://mjohnsonstories.net. She's also maryj59 on Twitter and BlueSky and mary-j-59 on livejournal and dreamwidth.

Molly Renee Kantz is an artist who works in a wide range of different mediums, including graphite pencil, pen and ink, oil paints, watercolors, and digital art. She's a graduate of The Texas Academy of Figurative Art, whose pieces can be found in some limited-edition prints, home-made postcards, and all of Prufrock's publications. When she's not drawing or painting she can be found either working in the garden, baking, or playing videogames on easy mode.

Danielle Krikorian graduated from Chapman University with a B.F.A in creative writing. She has an undying love for fairy tales and mythology and her short fiction piece, "Darci and the Hook, Line and Sinker" was published in the 2023 Fall Issue of *Open Minds Quarterly* and was also published in Issue #88: *The Art of Living by Kaleidoscope: Exploring the Experience of Disability through Literature and the Fine Arts.* She live in Southern California and works at Pretend City Children's Museum.

Adam Levine is a writer and attorney from Pittsburgh, now living and working in Los Angeles.

Annie McCann is an Indonesian-Australian writer and emcee based in Sydney, Australia. An avid reader of fantasy fiction stories inspired by cultural mythology, Annie has a passion for diverse voices and representation in books. When not writing, Annie emcees major pop culture conventions such as Supanova and Comic Con. Her debut short story *Twisted Elegance of the Deep Green Sea* a reimagining of a West Javanese, Indonesian legend is published in *This Fresh Hell* anthology. More of Annie's writing was recently acquired by Fictional Frontiers (US) which means we will see more from Annie including a full length novel soon.

Meg Moseman has been a fan of the Inklings since childhood. She lives in the mountains of Montana, where she works as a software engineer. In her spare time, she reads, writes, and illustrates fantasy and poetry. In addition to Lewis, Tolkien, and Williams, she loves Diana Wynne Jones, Kafka, Melville, Dickinson, and many others. Her poetry and art have appeared before in *Heroic Fantasy Quarterly* and *The Mythic Circle*.

J. Brice Odom is a writer from Macon, GA. He is the author of the short story collection *The Light of All Lights* and the poetry collection *Grain of Sand: Five Poems and the Chains of Camelot*. He has won recognition for flash fiction in the Almost an Inkling Contest and NYCmidnight Microfiction Contest. He considers himself just an older kid still telling stories. You can see more of his work at jbriceodom.com.

Holly Payne-Strange (she/her) is a novelist, poet and podcast creator. Her writing has been lauded by *USA Today*, *LA Weekly* and *The New York Times*. Additionally, she's given talks on podcast creation at Fordham University and The Player's Club. Her poetry has been published by various groups including *RedDoor, Door Is A Jar* magazine, *Call me [Brackets]*, and *Quail Bell Magazine*. She would like to thank her wife for all her support.

Daniel J. Pool is a librarian, film maker, and writer from the Southern Midwest. His work has appeared in *Farther Stars Than These*, the *Fringe Magazine*, and *Tavern Tall Tales*. He is a co-creator of the Double Issue Podcast.

A.J. Prufrock tells old-fashioned fantasy and fairy tales from a mythopoetic and mystical imagination (*ajprufrock.com*). The stories exist within and outside of time and will strike a chord with their heroic exploits large and small. "Pretty good but not as good as Narnia." –*Prufrock's Mom*

Dave Shortt is a long-time writer from the USA whose work has appeared over the years in a number of online and print literary-type venues, including *Uut Poetry, Sulfur*, and the print anthology *Octo-Emanations* https://www.amazon.com/Octo-Emanations-Carter-Kaplan/dp/B08GB7MLTY. More of his poems can be found in recent issues of *Unlikely Stories/Mark V, Coffin Bell, Mystic Owl*, and *Carmina Magazine*.

David Sparenberg, an international essayist, eco-poet, and storyteller, is author of four books: *EARTH KEEPER*: an Ecosophy of Poems; *EARTH CRISIS HUMAN CRISIS*: Urgent Essays; *BEING HERE & BELONGING*: Visions, Talks & Meditations, and *CONFRONTING the CRISIS*: Essays & Meditations on Eco Spirituality from Moon Books. David lives in Seattle, WA.

Robert Thomas studied classics, including Greek mythology, at the University of Toronto, and Roman history at Oxford. He writes poetry and short stories, the latter focussing on the unusual, horrific and macabre, and is currently working on an alternative history novel. He lives in Toronto, Canada, with his wife and son. He also likes camping and canoeing and cooking.

Ella Walsworth-Bell is known locally in Cornwall, South-West England, as the "mer-poet" for her love of all things ocean. She writes poetry and short stories exploring the interface of nature, love and myth-magic. She lives aboard a boat in the summer months with her family. Most recently, she curated two poetry anthologies, *Morvoren* and *Mordardh*, about sea swimming and surfing. Her short stories have been published in *Paperbound, Indigo Dreams, Cornwall: Secret and Hidden*. She came second in the *Perito Prize* with a story about inclusion and diversity, *Knitting for teenage boys*.

Editors' Introductions
by Victoria Gaydosik, with Nolan Meditz

Greetings, Subscribers, Contributors, and Readers, All, and welcome to the 2024 edition (issue #46) of *The Mythic Circle*, the creative writing publication of The Mythopoeic Society. With this issue, we continue the 37-year-long tradition (since 1987) of providing *The Mythic Circle* as a publishing outlet for members of The Mythopoeic Society and for writers and artists in the general public.

For this year's edition, it fell out that thirty artists--creative writers of poetry and fiction, along with creators of visual images--successfully brought their work to the attention of the staff of *The Mythic Circle*. It's always a chance as to what comes in over the electronic transom, and this year we received a wide range of enjoyable stories, poems, and images. For the first time in many years, the artist L. C. Atencio has once again provided front and back covers and an interior illustration all on mythic themes. The dragons on our covers echo the characters in *A Circle of Dragons,* which concludes our serial presentation of that novel of fairy-tale retellings by A. J. Prufrock. And the re-imagined story of Daphne from Greek mythology gets a folk-tale treatment in "The Tree," by Holly Payne-Strange, along with two illustrations of trees, by L. C. Atencio and Meg Moseman, also on a return visit to our pages. Additionally, Meg's poem "The Way" explores the difficulty of knowing how we should move through the world and through life.

More poems in this year's edition present mythic themes that include reminiscences of childhood imaginings ("Disenchantment," by Jacob Bier), an imagining of magical creatures emerging in the warmth of spring ("mushroom people," by a very long-time member of the Mythopoeic Society, Eleanor Farrell), a recollection of Stonehenge ("The Stone Circles at Avebury, England," by Dave Shortt), a prose-poem about love for the seat and center of life ("LOYAL to the EARTH," by David Sparenberg), and a poem celebrating life and its continuation ("To the Red Beacons," by Nicole Ai). The poet Holly Day returns to our pages with "Surrender," about the embrace of nature even after death. The Cornish poet and fiction writer Ella Walsworth-Bell also makes a return appearance in both forms with a poem about drawing strength from the ocean at dawn ("Seek Strength"), and with a story about a different, magical, and unbidden return to the sea, "Watermill Cove." And this year's poems also include a rare example of the Old English alliterative verse form so loved and used by J. R. R. Tolkien in "The War-Forge," by David Ehrenman.

The fiction selections for this issue begin and end in magic. Our opening story, "Dave's Birthday," by J. Brice Odom, is one of the happiest stories I've read in my tenure as editor of *The Mythic Circle*, mainly due to the joyous character of Dave. And our closing story, the conclusion of *A Circle of Dragons*, ends happily with the farmer's daughter outsmarting her dragon adversaries. In between, Jon Heggested retells a story in "Echo Still" that shows us the final stages of a woman's disappearance through her unrequited love for the handsome young man too in love with himself to notice her. Two coincidentally related stories show us different aspects of one long myth as we see the taming--and destruction--of the monster in "The Minotaur," by Robert Thomas, and the much later aftermath for Daedalus, the monster's creator, as he grieves his dead son Icarus in "Craftman's Bane," by S. R. Horgan. Adam Levine presents a modern-dress (and language and tech) Medusa in "An Ocean Away," and David Ehrenman introduces us to a heroine who might be a contemporary of Beowulf in "Melody of the Deep." Danielle Krikorian portrays the tragic scenario of the beginning of the end of the world in "All In: A Loki and Sigyn Tale." Several folktales are available such as "The Magician's Box," by Lawrence Buentello, "The Reluctant Monk," by Andoni Cossio, "The Moon Makes a Mockery," by Kevan Kenneth Bowkett, and a story of consequences,"You Mustn't Disquiet the Fauna," by Jared Bentley. An origin tale, "How the Moons Came to Be," comes from Mary Johnson, and a tale of an ending, "Dragon's Rest," is the work of Daniel J. Pool. And two stories show us supernatural protectors at work, "Grandmother Anna," by Kenneth Burtness, and the Javanese story "Rolling Gunung Tampomas," by Annie McCann.

Once again, I am grateful to Phillip Fitzsimmons for the images of his stained glass art.

We are very appreciative of the talented writers and artists who send their work to us for the recompence of a free paper copy of the journal. Please continue to support us with your creativity, and spread the word to other writers and artists of your acquaintance. Keep in mind that it is the policy of the journal to give preference to the members of The Mythopoeic Society, although we also accept submissions from the general public. Membership is affordable at $15.00; those wishing to join can make arrangements at https://www.mythsoc.org/join.htm. The Society's annual conference has been held in the summer for more than 50 years, and if you love fantasy and the works of the Inklings, you will find like-minded devotees there. This summer, our conference will be in Minneapolis, MN, in person for the 53rd time, with the theme "Fantasies of the Middle Lands," and registration is available at https://www.mythsoc.org/mythcon/mc53-reg.htm.

Until next summer, happy myth-making!

***Two Kittens*, by Phillip Fitzsimmons**

Dave's Birthday
by J. Brice Odom

Death comes for us all…well, everyone except Dave. It's not like Death hasn't tried, either. Death has tried to just take him, set traps for him, he very kindly stopped to wait for him, and once he even chased him down Main St. with his scythe. But Dave just wouldn't pay Death any mind. I think Death gave up, so Dave is still here.

Today is Dave's birthday.

His 167th birthday.

Dave loves his birthday. Unlike old people who like to ignore the fact they are getting older, Dave brags about it. If I were turning 167 years old, I'd brag too. He is pretty spry for his age, too. He still walks with a spring in his step and only carries a cane for his fashion sense. Some say it's cause he still does yoga every morning. It could be magic. When talking about Dave, it's best not to rule anything out.

Dave was looking dapper for his birthday. He was wearing a smooth black three piece suit with a slick black cane with a silver round handle at the top. His shoes were shined so perfectly Dave could see his face and mess of gray hair when he looked down at his toes.

At this point, Dave was a local celebrity. Dave's birthday had become the town festival. Forsyth had the Forsythia Festival, Sandersville had the Kaolin Festival, and the small town of Ashland had Dave's Birthday. The town square was covered in those folding canopies with merchants and artists hocking their hand-made wares. There was one of those spinning swing rides you usually see at carnivals. And, of course, there was a clown, too, making balloon animals for the boys and girls. The clown's giraffe was quite good.

Mama and Baby Giraffe photograph by Caroline Hunt
Stained Glass by Phillip Fitzsimmons

A little boy carrying one of those balloon giraffes was standing on the grass of the courthouse looking down the street. He saw all the tents and the merchants and the other children laughing and playing, but he was not laughing or playing. This little boy was searching. You see, Clifford Stanley had moved to Ashland with his mom and dad six months ago. He had heard the tales of this mad and impossibly old man, but he had never met Dave. Today, 6-year-old Clifford was determined to meet Dave.

This really all started a week ago. Mr. and Mrs. Stanley were good people. Mr. Stanley taught high school science and got a job at the high school. They moved here, though, because Mrs. Stanley got an engineering job at a nearby plant. They didn't know what to make of Dave. They didn't really believe the stories until they met Dave last Friday night.

The couple had gotten a babysitter and gone out for a date night. Now, date night for this couple did not mean putting on a nice coat and dress and going to eat horribly over-priced entrees. It meant going out to listen to live music and drinking a few beers and just walking around and laughing until it was time to go home.

Well, the final bar they ended up that night was having karaoke. The Stanleys are very happy you are reading this and can't hear their terrible singing voices warbling "Don't Go Breaking My Heart." But regardless of the quality of their voices, the couple had a blast. After smiling and getting beet red on stage, the two sat down and listened to good songs sung badly. That's a bit unfair. A couple of the people up there did know how to sing. Mr. Stanley stopped drinking early enough so he could drive his wife home safely when the night was over. Mrs. Stanley had a couple more after that point. As they got ready to leave and were putting on their coats, the MC jumped back up on the stage.

"Ladies and gents! Before you go, we have one last surprise! We are adding a last performer to the list tonight, because we just couldn't say no! Everybody on your feet for Ashland's very own Dave!"

And this man who seemed both old and oddly young came bounding up on stage as the room went nuts. He was holding a cane he clearly didn't need. It was clear he didn't need it because he was twirling it as he walked. He hadn't even started yet, but the crowd was on its feet hootin' and hollerin'. Dave's smile went ear to ear and he gave a big wave to the crowd. He centered himself up to the microphone and used a hand to quickly fix his white hair to part the right way. It didn't work too well. Never did. His hair always looked a little disheveled.

Dave boomed into the mic, "How you doing, Ashland, Georgia?"

The crowd yelled back.

Dave didn't stop smiling. He caught a glimpse of someone and pointed and waved at them. He looked over the crowd again. "Glad to see y'all are all having a good time. Y'all don't mind if I sing a last song do y'all?"

The crowd cheered their approval.

Mr. and Mrs. Stanley were amused and bewildered by the whole scene.

The first strains of "Don't Stop Believing" started coming out of the speaker and this old man's voice poured into the microphone. The only word that Mr. Stanley could come up with later to describe the voice was pure. The crowd swayed. Lighters were held up. And every time he got back to the refrain the whole joint joined in. Mr. and Mrs. Stanley were swept along in the euphoria. Dave closed the placed down and they all danced out to their cars. I don't mean they walked out to their cars with a spring in their step. They actually danced out to their cars. Mr. and Mrs. Stanley made it back to the car and took one look at each other. Then they smiled and burst out laughing. They laughed for a good ten minutes before finally driving home to relieve the babysitter.

Young Clifford heard his parents talking about their experience the next morning while eating his cereal. Mrs. Stanley said that when Dave went up on stage the whole thing felt like magic. Clifford heard the word "magic" and his imagination began to turn. This Dave was real. He was the man whom Death could not catch and who used magic wherever he went. In Clifford's mind, that made Dave a wizard. He had to meet a wizard.

So, on Dave's Birthday, Clifford was not laughing and playing with the other children. He was searching.

He was going to find his wizard.

He told his green balloon giraffe, whom he had named Robert, that it was time to go search. He saw Mom and Dad talking to a friend of theirs, and he slipped away with Robert to start their adventure.

Clifford weaved through the legs of adults moving here and there. To him they were giants blocking his path, but Clifford and Robert deftly avoided the terrible gargantuans who at any moment could carry him away—well, back to his parents, anyway.

Clifford was looking for a sign.

A sign. Some kind of sign.

And then Clifford caught sight of something between all the legs and past the tents. It was shining gold on a tree. He pushed by the tablecloths as he slipped between two merchant booths. Clifford held Robert up so he could see, too.

"Robert, look. It's a sign."

And it was. Not something metaphorical. An actual sign.

It was nailed to the tree. It had a gold border. The gold had glitter in it to give it an extra shine. The sign had big red letters on it:

Dave's Birthday
All Day Party
Dave will be at:

The Dunking booth
The Hot Dog Eating Contest
The Music Stage

…and, of course, wherever else he shows up!

The boy smiled as he read the sign. His parents just had told him they were going downtown. He didn't know anything about what was happening today until now.

The boy looked at his giraffe, "Robert! We can find Dave now!"

About that moment, Clifford noticed growing commotion. There were shouts. He didn't catch what they said, but Clifford could tell it was not good.

Then one voice stood out. It was his mother's voice, "Clifford! Where are you?"

There were other voices crying his name, too. All asking where he was. Clifford didn't really understand why there was a worry. He hadn't gone anywhere, after all. He was still at Dave's Birthday Party with everyone else. He thought about running toward the dunking booth since he knew where that was. But Clifford's adventurous streak had a weakness. He was a good boy.

Clifford held onto his giraffe and went back through the booths to the middle of the road. "I'm right here, Mom!"

As his Mom scooped up and hugged him, he noticed the whole crowd seemed to breathe a sigh of relief. The boy had been found. He didn't understand the worry of a parent over a missing child. He did understand that he still hadn't found Dave.

"Can we go to the Dunking Booth?" Clifford used Robert to point in the direction of the carnival game.

His Mom looked at him quizzically and Clifford repeated the question as his relieved father joined them.

His parents looked at each other and shrugged their shoulders. "Sure, Clifford."

His Mom put him back down and they continued to walk, but Clifford's mom kept a hold of his hand this time.

They got to the Dunking Booth and there was a long line waiting to throw and a good crowd watching. There was laughter and good cheer. Some of the people in the crowd were starting to drift away. Clifford was looking for Dave and his magic, but as he listened to the conversations passing him by, he sagged so that Robert almost touched the rough asphalt that would have surely destroyed the giraffe. Clifford knew he was too late.

Listening to the adults above him, he discovered he had certainly missed a scene.

"Man, Dave is having a blast today."

"Why shouldn't he? It's his birthday!"

"I knew this Dunking Booth wasn't going to be simple when he said he was going to be the target."

"I know, right? Can you believe he had a box of tomatoes up there with him?"

"He was taunting everyone. 'You're sad, man. You couldn't hit the target if I brought it over there to you!' I swear every tomato he threw hit the thrower."

"They needed a dunk in the tank more than Dave did." Laughter surrounded all the words Clifford was hearing from down at their knees. Apparently, the only reason Dave got wet was because he jumped in at the end. The tomatoes and trash-talk had worked. No one had knocked him in the water.

Clifford pondered this scene and could see the scene in his mind, but not Dave. It was an empty space in the story. Clifford saw a sign pointing in the direction of the eating contest. Since his Mom was still holding his hand, he started tugging her in the direction of the next place that Dave would be.

Clifford's parents were getting grumpy. Clifford felt it. He started to feel small, smaller than his small height. He started to feel angry. Couldn't they just let him go find Dave?

"Now, hold on a second. First you run off and then you bring us over here so you can watch people fall in the water, but as soon as we are here you want to leave." Clifford's Dad did something that perhaps he did not think much of, but to Clifford meant the world. His Dad looked off for a moment, frustration visible on his face to all who knew him, especially his child. Then he took a deep breath and let that go. Looked down at his son with a slight smile. "What is it that you really want, Clifford?"

At the question, Clifford was restored to his natural size. A smile spread on his face, reflecting back to his father. "I want to see Dave."

"You could have said that in the first place. Come on." And now his father led them down the path to the stage for the Hot Dog Eating Contest. People were gathered around a raised platform with a red curtain behind it. The platform was wide but not deep. There was a table for five people and a pyramid of hotdogs in front of each chair. An MC introduced the first four contestants, three men and one woman. They emerged from behind the red curtain and took their seats. They all had a plastic bib on that wasn't much more than a garbage bag. There was a drum roll starting.

"Good afternoon, Ashland, on this wonderful day. This wonderful birthday. The man of the hour is here. He is here to take on these four fine challengers. He has won for the last 10 years. He has won 17 of the 20 of these that we have held. Today is his 167th birthday. Dave!"

The crowd cheered wildly when he bounded up from behind the curtain. He was wearing dry clothes now, though his hair was still wet and slicked back. He had a navy blue sports coat on, but underneath he was wearing a tee-shirt with Pink Floyd's Dark Side of the Moon cover on it and a pair of jeans. He smiled from ear to ear and he waved with both hands. The crowd serenaded him with Happy Birthday. He placed his hand over and tapped his heart to express his gratitude, and then he shook his opponents' hands.

To the crowd he shouted, "Shall we begin?"

They cheered back, "Yes!"

A whistle blew and the clock started. The five contestants started to eat as fast as they could. Mr. and Mrs. Stanley looked across the whole table. It was a disgusting display. The hot dogs were being scarfed down in almost continuous eating. Their stomachs didn't like it, but their eyes would not dare miss a moment.

Clifford, on the other hand, was watching one man. Dave. At last. He was there in front of him. Clifford had grandparents. He knew old people. And this man in front of him was something entirely different. He was unquestionably old. The wrinkles on his face were deep. His hands thin. His hair nothing but white. Dave's whole body seemed like he could turn to the side and Clifford would only see a line. Yet, none of that matter. He moved as if he were in his twenties. His hands moved with speed as he ate one dog after another. He slowed for not a moment and when the bell ring he swallowed the last hot dog from his pyramid. The woman was just about five dogs behind, but he smoked the men by a mile. He jumped to his feet and, with a large belch, he smiled again and raised both hands in the air. The other eaters looked like they were ready to sleep on the table.

"Robert, it is magic."

That word magic again echoed in Clifford's mind. His eyes stayed on Dave until he disappeared behind the curtain. Clifford wanted to go meet him, but his Mom was still holding his hand. She wasn't going to let go. Suddenly, Dave emerged from behind the curtain, and the crowd cheered again. He jumped down from the stage and shook hands and high fived the still giddy crowd as he made his way through. About the moment Dave was to burst through the crowd near the enraptured young boy, Clifford dropped Robert and the giraffe's brief life was ended beneath the unsuspecting foot of Dave.

The pop caused Dave to stop and look down, and he saw the face of the stricken little boy. Clifford's eyes were wide and tears were welling in them. His lip was quivering. He wanted to shout and cry, but he was trying to hold back. He failed. The tears fell drop, drop, drop upon the earth. The tears fell in the midst of torn balloon rubber that had moments ago been a giraffe. And then a wail escaped his lips.

Dave, for the first time on this birthday, stopped smiling. He knelt down until he was eye level with the boy and he gave him a hug.

"Shhh. Shhh. I'm so sorry, young man." He let go of the boy and looked him in the tearful eyes. Looking up at Clifford's parents. "What's your boy's name?"

"Clifford."

His gaze returned to the crying boy. "Ah, Clifford, but hold on a second." The twinkle returned to Dave's eye as he swept up Robert's remains with his hands. "Maybe there is something I can do. Did it have a name?"

"H-h-his name was Robert." Clifford wiped some of the tears from his face.

"Good name. Robert is a strong giraffe name." Dave started to roll the pieces around in hands and he stood up. "Oh yes, I know just the ticket."

This 167-year-old-miracle of a man put the balloon pieces in his coat pocket and jumped and turned around three times then clapped his hands. He knelt back down to Clifford. And from his coat pocket he pulled a green stuffed giraffe the same size as the one he had popped.

"Robert has come back to you better than ever. Death couldn't quite catch him, either. Just like me. Sorry you had to go through that." Dave smiled at Clifford.

Clifford's mouth dropped. Well, so did the mouth of every adult around who could see. The boy held the green giraffe and pulled it into a hug. Dave rustled the boy's hair a little, shook Mr. and Mrs. Stanley's hands, and then, with a spring in his step, walked on to the rest of his Birthday Party.

The Stanleys made it home eventually, but Clifford hadn't said a word. In his head a single word kept repeating. As he laid down to sleep with Robert close at his side, just before his eyes closed for the night, the word finally escaped his lips.

"Magic."

Magic it must have been, but Clifford and Dave did not cross paths again for some time. Three months' time, in fact. It was another birthday. This time it was Clifford's birthday. In the meantime, Clifford and Robert, for the giraffe was rarely far from his hand, had heard some further stories of Dave's exploits around town.

Mrs. Stanley had gone to the grocery store one day and Dave was manning the cash register. Seems he had come in to buy some cereal, and the cashier, who was pregnant, needed to get off her feet. Unfortunately, she was the only one working because the other cashier had called in sick. She was about to fall over—she was so tired. Dave steadied her, sat her in a chair, and started running the register. It was a rush at the store, but he kept everyone moving through the line, and the woman got to just sit there and take some deep breaths for a long while. He even got the long line to sing with him when random songs popped into his head which included "We Will Rock You" and "Unanswered Prayers." Eventually the cashier's shift ended and Dave handed the register over to the new person. Finally, he paid for his cereal and went home two hours after he walked in the door.

A few weeks later, Mr. Stanley ran into Dave at the public golf course. Dave was a walk up. No reservation. He had woken up that morning and decided it was a golf day, so he showed up. It was a booked day, but Mr. Stanley's group only had three players so Dave joined with them. Dave and the men talked about sports and the ups and downs that come with life all the time, but Dave worked into their conversation literature, philosophy, science, space, and art here and there. Mr. Stanley said he hardly realized it had happened at all because Dave just had a way of talking. He also had a way of playing. Dave birdied the first 17 holes and only missed out on 18 birdies because the putt lipped out on the last hole. He shook their hands at the end of the round and bought them all a beer in the clubhouse. He wished them all a wonderful day when he finished his beer and departed.

Somewhere in those rambling golf course conversations, Mr. Stanley must have mentioned that Clifford's birthday was coming up because the celebration for Clifford's 7th birthday arrived, and Dave knocked on the door with a giant cake.

"Happy Birthday, Clifford!"

The cake had a large green giraffe on it and seven candles. Each candle was in the shape of a number. When Dave put the cake down to light the candles. He started with the candle shaped like the number one and worked up to the seven. And of course, "Happy Birthday" was sung as Clifford blew out the candles. Clifford smiled the whole time and held Robert the giraffe close to his side.

Clifford opened his gifts, and there were all the wonderful things one would suspect a 7-year-old boy to love. There was a baseball glove and ball. There were action figures and Legos. A movie that came out last summer. Mrs. Stanley also made sure there was a book of some kind, as she always did, amongst the many gifts.

While the adult Stanleys took care of their guests, Dave sat at the table across from Clifford. The other children there were playing with the party favors and didn't notice that the birthday boy, in fact, had watched Dave intensely from the moment he crossed the threshold. Dave leaned down and put his face on his hands so his face was even with Clifford's.

"How are you enjoying your birthday?"

7

Clifford studied Dave's face. This was the magic man here before him. He wasn't really sure why. "It's good."

Dave returned the favor and studied Clifford's face. But whereas Clifford was looking for answers, Dave just enjoyed the moment. A bemused smirk was on his face as he watched the curious and guarded boy. "How is Robert doing?" He nodded his head at the stuffed green giraffe.

"He's good." Clifford still wasn't sure of his situation.

"Is good the only word you know?" There was a twinkle in Dave's eye.

Clifford shook his head and let a soft laugh out.

Dave narrowed his eyes just a tad. "I think you want to ask me questions."

And there was a pause.

Then Clifford let the dam break. "Are you really 167 years old? How are you so old? Did Death really chase you down the road? What do you do? How did you make Robert? Do you have any family? How did you end up in Ashland? Do you like being so old? Do you like baseball? What is your favorite movie?" Then his little blue eyes darted back and forth to think if he left anything out and his eyes widened. "Are you really magic?"

Dave let silence hang in the air for a moment, and then he laughed. It was not a mocking laugh, but warm and good natured. His face communicated nothing but warmth. He leaned forward and started answering Clifford's questions. Some of the answers were straight forward. Yes, he loved baseball, and some old black-and-white movie Clifford had never heard of, Casa-something, was his favorite one. Yes, he had been married and even had a kid, but they had all passed long ago. Some of the answers Clifford did not understand. He wasn't sure if Dave admitted to being magical or just was being fanciful. There was something about a swan in a lake on a beautiful sunny day and a woman in a white robe. Dave swore that Death did chase him down the street once, and he laughed as he ran. Clifford chuckled at it all and his eyes lit up.

With the questions answered, Clifford ran off to play with the other children, who were starting to think he must be in trouble since he was still sitting at the table with an adult. Dave watched with gladness for a moment before going to talk with the adults in the kitchen. Then he slipped away to whatever his next event of the day was.

Dave made a point of being friends with the Stanleys. They were invited to dinner and Clifford became so used to the magic of Dave that it was just a part of life. A good part of life. A part that made him smile, but he was no longer obsessed with the idea of the 167-year-old man. He just was happy to see him because it was Dave. Mr. Stanley and Clifford watched the Opening Day Braves game at Dave's house for the next several years.

As for so many of us, these truly happy times were not to last forever. Just after Dave's 176th Birthday Party, Mrs. Stanley got a promotion, but the job was at another plant, and the Stanleys who had been brought to Ashland by a company were sent away by it.

The farewell party was a big affair. Dave saw to that. Still hopping around like he always did, the old man put a stage on their front lawn in the middle of the night and there was one band after another all day from when the sun came up. It seemed half the town came by at some time or another. Dave and Clifford sang a duet of "Bohemian Rhapsody" that had everyone singing with them too. Family and friends went inside to eat hot dogs and burgers and the stage was gone when they began to leave. There were tears as all said their goodbyes to friends who had come so unexpectedly and were leaving much too soon.

When the car pulled out of the driveway the next day just after the moving truck had left, Dave gave them all a big hug and told them to come see him anytime, and not to forget his Birthday.

And they didn't.

Not for a long while anyway. Each year Dave saw Clifford get bigger as he finished school and started a career. He watched gray sneak into the hair of Mr. Stanley and Mrs. Stanley. Then one year they had to miss the Birthday. They called to apologize and wish him well. Then Mr. and Mrs. Stanley came, but Clifford couldn't get leave from his job. The next year Clifford came but not his parents. Then it was a few years before Mr. and Mrs. Stanley were able to get back. Then the next year he heard nothing.

Dave did not slow down and there were always new friends and he was still having fun, but he always noticed when friends drifted away and never forgot them.

His 199th birthday had arrived and the party was as big as ever. Dave won a pie eating contest and judged a chili cook off that included some Carolina Reaper. But not even that reaper was effective against Dave. At the end of a long wonderful day, he sat in a chair in his home. And there was a knock on the door.

Bounding down the hall, Dave answered the door.

Before him stood Clifford.

And a small boy, too, holding a worn stuffed green giraffe with an eye missing.

Clifford smiled but not ear to ear. "Hi, Dave."

The nearly 200-year-old man gave him a hug without a second thought and the scooped the little boy up. "You must be Clifford's little boy. What's your name?"

A little taken aback, the small child managed his name eventually. "Cecil."

That ever-present twinkle in Dave's eye seemed to work its magic. "I'm glad to meet you, Cecil. I'm an old friend of your father's. My name is Dave."

The child smiled back and the father and son were invited in. The three went to the den. Dave fixed a couple drinks and gave Cecil a Coke. Dave and Clifford sat across from each other as Cecil held his giraffe and studied this strange man, much as his father had years ago.

"It's been a long time, Clifford, but I am so happy you have come by."

Clifford seemed to grimace more than smile.

Dave looked at him with concern. "What's the matter, dear boy?"

There were tears in Clifford's eyes though he was trying to keep them from falling. "It's my parents. They're gone. There was a car accident. And that was it."

Clifford stared into space. Dave was in front of him, but Clifford stared through him at nothing.

Dave's light receded from his face for a moment. "I am so sorry, Clifford. What can I do?"

"It hurts every day. I just wanted to talk. How do you do this? You have lived so long. You must have lost enough people by now. How is this immortality not a curse? How can you be okay with living forever when everyone else dies?" Clifford, at last, looked Dave in the eye.

Dave looked at the ground and took a deep breath. He looked over at Cecil and then back at Clifford. The twinkle in his eye had returned and his soft smile was as warm as the sun.

"I've never understood why people thought this was a curse. Everyone always does. There is Tuck and the mummies and the vampires and Dorian Gray. Immortality is always treated like a poison. I never understood."

Clifford's head tilted a bit to the side, studying the visage that had so fascinated him as a boy. "How can you bear to lose people over and over?"

"It never gets easy, Clifford. I loved my wife more than anything in this world. She died when I was 50 years old. Cancer took those blue eyes that held my soul. There was never another woman for me. Our son lived until he was 92. He lived a good life. But I remained. Those were the worst times of my life. And there have been plenty of other terrible days. Like right now." Tears sat in the corners of his eyes. "But with each person, I see another bit of creation. Another bit of the divine. I have always taken joy in people. Simple joy in watching people live the small moments of the day. Moments like a small boy trying to understand the strangeness of the world and people around him. And those small moments are their own kind of magic."

Clifford smiled genuinely for the first time.

Dave returned the smile. His twinkling eye somehow brighter. "What I have is a blessing, Clifford. I love all these people and the world they weave together. I've got to stay. I don't want to miss anything. I want to see what happens next. And today may be filled with sorrow, which is right," Dave looked down at Cecil, "but joy will come with what happens next."

Clifford looked down at his son as well. The sorrow was not gone, but the weight seemed lighter. Dave and Clifford talked for hours over all the things of life. Clifford promised to come visit again soon and bring his wife for Dave to meet.

As they said their goodbyes at the door, Cecil held Robert the giraffe tightly. Dave looked at the good old stuffed animal. "Cecil, what has happened to Robert's eye?"

The little boy said it fell off.

"That is too bad, but hold on a second." Dave put his hands together and blew into them. He rubbed them together and cracked his knuckles, then he placed his hands over Robert's head and blew into his hands again before pulling them away. "Ah, that's better."

And there, perfectly matching, was Robert's second eye. Cecil's mouth hung open. Clifford laughed and said good-bye one last time before getting in the car and driving off.

Cecil, finally, broke his silence from the back seat. "How did he do that?"

Clifford looked into the rearview mirror at his amazed little boy with a smile twinkling with Dave's light. "Magic."

Surrender
by Holly Day

The tree sends its roots down into the soil, wraps around
the woman lying just beneath the soil. It's as if the tree
has taken her in its arms, so slowly, so carefully,
that she's turned to mulch long before the embrace is completed.
But time works differently when you're dead, or you're a tree.

When the stump is dug up years later, after the tree's been felled and the soil's been tilled
the man who bought the land for his house marvels
at how the knot of roots and filaments uncovered by his plow
looks just like the outline of a woman, so carefully has the tree wrapped itself
around her body over the years, even after everything of her is gone
the flesh, her bones, even the thin fabric of her blue cotton dress
even so, she has been remembered.

LOYAL to the EARTH
by David Sparenberg

LOYAL to the EARTH

If you choose loyalty, bypass being merely patriotic. Patriotism is a political tool used mostly by propagandists to stir emotions and further an oppositional agenda—an ideology.

Loyalty is a keystone quality or virtue of moral character— empathy, honesty, courage, perseverance, and loyalty. Character shows up in patterns across the variables of situations. Moral character is existential. When tested it becomes defining. Through moral character (the Eye of the Heart) a person evaluates the consequences of their action.

Be loyal to the Earth. Apply the Gandhian directive to think globally while acting locally. Local is where you are. It is your home turf. It is where you nest.

From your spot, Earth goes out and on in all directions. And everywhere where Earth is, there is life. Life happens. Because Earth is a life place.

Choose life. As much as you can, do so with the strength and wealth of moral character. Choose loyalty to the Earth. The Earth is foundational. It is where life makes life happen.
We are of the event. Behind the event is the process. We are part of the process.

The Tree
By Holly Payne-Strange

She hoped for rain. It was really the only thing that soothed her, that eased the pain in her limbs, the creaking of her sides. Her roots went deep now. So deep that when they eventually felled her for timber, as she knew they would, they would have to rip and claw at the earth itself to get those last parts of her. That made her smile. It made the many months, almost years now, that she has been standing there entirely worth it.

Her face was still soft and smooth, she still had long dark hair that fluttered and twisted in the breeze. In fact, all the way down to her shoulders was supple flesh, and she still felt her neck was quite shapely, considering the rest of her body. She had the feeling that if she wanted to, really wanted to, she could break this enchantment and walk away, go back to the human she once was. Her legs were hardened with bark, bound together with gnarled wood, but some days she could still feel the twitch of her knee underneath it all.

She didn't want to move. Didn't want to be human.

Trees Overhead, by Meg Moseman

She wanted to wait. It was there they had decided to meet; her and her lover, Althea Kallistrata. Or just Kali to those who knew her well. They had promised to meet at the crossroads, under the full moon, ready to run away together and start a new life. Melisande had shown up. Kallistrata had not.

But it hadn't really mattered to Melisande. She wasn't sure if she simply had never expected Kali to show up in the first place--and so felt no disappointment--or perhaps, if she still believed that she would, one day, show up--and so felt no disappointment, even now.

Either way, she was content. She had waited so long, her patience had been so enduring, that she became part of the landscape. She first noticed it when a tiny sprout blossomed from her ankle, a little green shoot, so small it could almost be called cute. It enchanted her. Somehow, she just knew what it needed; roots, sunlight, stability. Everything she had wanted with Kali, everything she knew she was capable of. And so she gave it to the little tree instead.

She didn't quite understand at first. Didn't realize that it would become her, consume her. But she didn't mind either, passively accepting it when her choices became clear. Even at this cost, she wouldn't leave. She chose a nice spot near the crossroads. Close to the road, so she could have company from passing travelers, but not too near any other trees so they didn't have to compete for resources. With a good view of the harbor, where she could see the temple slowly being erected, marble pillar by marble pillar.

And so, she saw the man long before he saw her, his toga flapping in the breeze. At first, she didn't think he was coming in her direction; only weary traders and long-distance travelers crossed by this road, laden down with their goods, usually with pack mules and servants. He came completely alone, bearing nothing. He had come solely to see her.

"Hello," he said sheepishly, as he came under her shade. He had kind eyes and a sweet smile, slightly out of breath from his long hike.

"Hello," she smiled back, only mildly curious at the stranger before her.

"I've heard you're an expert in love," he started.

She actually laughed, throwing her head back, her leaves fluttering with the unfamiliar sound. "Who told you that?" She asked. Apparently, her story had spread quite far, a fact she was at least a little proud of. Good, she thought, people should know her devotion. It was impressive. *She* was impressive.

"I'd like your help," the young man said. "I…I have a similar problem. My love is leaving today, following her family to another village across the island. And I don't know if she'll be back." Here his voice broke. "And I don't know how I can live with that. Please. Help me."

"Of course I'll help, if I can," she said, looking down at him with pity. "But honestly, I don't know what I can do." She longed to reach down and touch his face, though that ability was lost to her now, sacrificed instead to the birds that nested in her branches.

He eyed her. "Have you tried?"

"Tried what?" she asked, "I just met you."

"No, I know, but have you tried…doing things? Like in the stories? You know, how some druids can cultivate diamonds, or illusionists can capture the stars. Things like that."

In truth, she had not tried. It hadn't even occurred to her.

"Would you mind?" he asked. "Can you, I don't know…make a flower grow or something?"

She blushed. In truth she'd rather not have an audience for her first attempt. She'd rather perfect it, whip the magic out when it was ready to dazzle and amaze, to make people cheer and applaud. But she supposed she had no choice. It was a good idea after all, and she wasn't rude enough to ask him to leave. Closing her eyes and taking a deep breath, she gathered her….energy, or something, she wasn't quite sure. She felt it pulsating in her trunk, beating throughout her body like a heartbeat she'd only just discovered.

In a burst of light, hyacinths shot from the ground, bright pink against the green grass, growing and blooming in mere moments. She gasped in joy, trying it again and again. Red poppies and purple roses joined the cacophony of color, creating a blanket of petals in front of her, spilling out like an aisle before a throne.

"I did it!" she shrieked, mind suddenly ablaze with other possibilities.

The man smiled at her, seemingly as happy as she was.

"That was incredible," he gushed, bending down to smell a rose. "They are totally indistinguishable from the real thing."

"They are real," she said with a sudden confidence.

Ma Vie D'arbre by L.C. Atencio

"Of course, I meant…anyway." Here he took a deep breath, standing tall and looking into her eyes with a sudden defiance. "I'd still like your help. My love, Elysia, she has to pass through here. Her cart is old and rickety, and she always sits on top of it. I keep telling her it's dangerous, but she never listens to me, I—anyway. That's not important. If you shoot one of your roots out, I'm sure you can topple the cart."

"Make her fall?" Melisande guessed.

"Just enough to break a leg. Then she won't be able to travel. Then she'll have to come home with me."

She stared down at him, shocked that she wasn't appalled at the plan. That she was intrigued.

"The timing would have to be immaculate."

"I think you're up to the challenge."

It occurred to her that maybe she should ask why this woman was not interested in the passionate, handsome young man before her. A man who clearly adores her and would do anything to win her heart. But she also realized that she didn't care. That love, to her, was a twisted and gnarled thing, more a wild force to be tamed than a delicate butterfly--or whatever the poets were saying these days.

She smiled, wanting to protect this man from all the hurt in all the world, wanting to give him his heart's desire. Suddenly feeling confident that she could, and proud of her generosity.

"You should hide somewhere. Go home. But take the roses with you, take some by the root and plant them in your garden."

The man beamed at her, happy to take her advice. He left, and Melisande waited. But it was a different kind of waiting now, a deeper, darker waiting. A yearning that she knew would be fulfilled--so different from her own, fruitless days. It felt good.

As soon as she saw the cart, she knew it was the right one. It was exactly as described, with an almost impossibly pretty girl on top, long hair blowing in the breeze.

Melisande struck at just the right moment, just when the cart was going down a hill, picking up speed, until—

Crash! Everything went flying, the people, the goods, the cart. The girl, whatever her name was, Melisande had forgotten, lay sprawled on the side of the road, her leg twisted, her eyes bright with pain, face curled in a scream. Melisande smiled, feeling simply that she had won.

It was the last thing she saw. Perhaps it was the sudden burst of magic, or perhaps some part of her had fully, finally committed to the tree. But there was no going back. Bark sprang up around her, consuming her neck, her face, her whole head, shooting upwards and into the sky in a joyous explosion of leaves and blossoms.

Her metamorphosis was complete. She finally felt free.

In the years that came, the villagers would often comment about how unlucky it was that the transformation (which had obviously been a long time coming) would finalize at that moment. But of course, it had brought the young lovers together again, so there was a silver lining. Making the best out of something bad. In fact, they thought it was rather gallant how the young man had stepped up to take care of his now wife. They got married that same month, house decorated with purple roses and red poppies, scenting the air with an odor that Elysia could never get rid of. She knew her husband loved those roses and so would never complain, though she had the strangest feeling that each year the plant had more thorns and fewer blooms. That sometimes, it even changed depending on who was looking at it. It never cut her husband the way it did her.

But of course, that was such a crazy thought. She would never assume she was important enough for magic, real magic, to touch her life. What kind of person would be arrogant enough to think that?

The Magician's Box
by Lawrence Buentello

During the twentieth year of the reign of King Thomas, fearfully referred to in the provinces as "Bloody Tom," His Highness found an interest in conjurers and magicians as amusement in the court, conscripting many such personages from every corner of the lands for his entertainment. He required conscription, of course, because no sane conjurer would volunteer to display his craft before so capricious a sovereign, as the king's sadistic whims were well known by his subjects.

Failing to adequately entertain our king often resulted in imprisonment, torture, or death—for he was a vicious man more mercenary than monarch. After his wife, our queen, had died of doubtful causes, he sent his only son, the prince, into the custody of monks across the realm, divorcing himself of the memory of his wife and his fatherly duties in one swift proclamation.

As his majesty's latest chamberlain, I had been charged with gathering these entertainers to stand before their king to show their gifts. And one by one, failing to astound our "Bloody Tom," who felt compelled to denounce their manipulations by exposing their 'secrets' through his own knowledge of trickery, these magicians met an end commensurate with the degree of his annoyance.

And since not one of these men presented by his chamberlain had once amused the king, he lately suggested that if I didn't present to him some legitimate conjurer of the realm, and very soon, I would join their upbraided company in the grave.

Moved to action by his imperative, and determined to avoid the pit, I scoured the lands for a worthy practitioner of the arts, and soon declared his demand to be met. The day came, and then the evening, when I stood before my king in his court as usher to a miracle.

"What fool have you procured for our bemusement this evening?" our sovereign bade me from his throne, a great carven chair fixed with precious stones and gilding. He touched his scarlet robes and purple vestments casually, though his dark eyes fixed me with a foreboding stare. "Our hope is for a wondrous exhibition, lest we are forced by disappointment to seek the services of yet *another* chamberlain."

I bowed respectfully, first to the sovereign on the throne, then to the seated courtiers, then to the quiet ladies sitting discomfited in the shadows. "For your joy alone, Your Highness, I have found the finest magician in these lands. Perhaps in all the world!"

King Thomas laughed. "You give yourself no quarter for mistaken impressions. Is this man truly the greatest conjurer in the world?"

I bowed again, shielding my eyes in subservience. "I have myself witnessed the glory of his art, Your Grace, and must vouch for his mastery of the craft of conjuration. By my life, I swear this is true!"

A general utterance rose in the audience, for all those seated in the royal hall understood the implications of my failing to deliver to our 'Bloody Tom' all I had promised. But by my eternal soul, I spoke the truth, though of the nature of that truth I was not willing, in the moment, to explicate.

"Very well, our chamberlain," the king said measuredly. "If this man does not prove by me to be the best conjurer in the world I will have you both locked in chains and left for rats."

I said nothing more but bowed again and moved into the shadows.

Presently, on the sounding of horns, a frail old man stepped into the torchlight of the hall, a thin white beard depending from his chin and an aged leather cloak embracing his shoulders. He moved before the throne, bowing reverently before our frowning king, then spread his bony arms and smiled.

"I am Old James," the magician said, "and I've come to amaze and delight you! For I hold the secrets of the magical arts!"

The king's anger shone brightly on his face. "You are a peasant in rags! Where is your costuming, your staff, your cap?" Now King Thomas turned his gaze upon me where I stood. "Do you seek to insult me with this rogue? Why do you bring a beggar before me?"

"Sire," I said calmly, my hands folded in supplication, "he is no beggar. He truly is the greatest magician in the land."

"Your Majesty," the old man said, "if you would let me prove my skills to you then you will surely understand."

"Very well," our sovereign capitulated, turning his attention once again to the old magician. "But pray your skills are worthy of my praise, for if you fail to show yourself as the finest magician of the *world* I shall watch you and my chamberlain perish in flames for your impudent lies."

The threat of dying by fire failed to impress any fear upon the old man's face. He merely nodded, bowed, and gestured toward the hall's great doors.

Immediately four soldiers moved into the hall carrying between them a large wooden box, ten-foot square, with each side affixed with a latched door. As the king carefully assessed this device, the soldiers left the large box standing before the throne before retreating.

The old magician moved before the door on the box facing the king, pulled the latch and opened it. Without a word, he then stepped to each side of the wooden box opening each door in turn, leaving all the doors open for the king's perusal. As all could see, when all the doors were opened the cavity lay empty, enclosed only by a wooden ceiling, but bereft of contents. The old man stepped to the far door and let King Thomas appraise him by line of sight through the box. Then the magician closed and latched all the doors again before addressing our sovereign.

"As Your Highness has witnessed for himself," the old man said, "this simple cube of wood lies unpopulated, for by its magic nature, imbued within its structure by my arts, no thing may exist within it but leave this earth forever. This claim I shall prove to you this eventide by stepping into this wondrous device and vanishing before your eyes!"

"Your claim is a bold one," King Thomas said. "Pray you keep your word. Should you fail to dematerialize before us, you will find yourself *burning* within your own magical device."

The old man only smiled before turning to the large wooden box, opening the facing door and stepping inside. Then he closed the door, lost to our sight.

As the king, his courtiers, his guards, and his chamberlain stood waiting in the dancing firelight, not a sound could be heard disturbing our expectations.

Then the king, gesturing toward me in agitation, cried, "Let us end this foolishness, our chamberlain. Open the doors of this device!"

I obeyed his command, moving from side to side of the box, pulling latches and opening doors before the expectant gazes of all seated in the hall. The box stood empty; the old man had vanished!

From all four sides of the box, the startled audience confirmed its untenanted status, and even King Thomas stood away from his throne in wonder. The old magician had disappeared before our eyes, having no opportunity to deceive us by stealth, for at no time had his device stood unobserved.

The king, quite unnerved by the spectacle, stepped down from his dais and approached the box. "This is only a trick!" he declared, though his expression betrayed his surprise.

"Old James truly kept the secrets of the universe," I suggested gently, gesturing toward the empty box. "Do you not believe this by your own eyes?"

King Thomas regarded my impudence with a haughty stare, though too absorbed by the mystery to address my challenge to his authority. "I will expose the method of your magician's deception, our chamberlain. Then let you and Old James use his magic to escape perdition!"

As all within the great hall watched, the king circumnavigated the box, touching the framework analytically, gazing thoughtfully into the dark recess.

"The old man hides within," he declared, spurred by his need to display his inimitable intellectual qualities, "disguised by treacherous carpentry."

"You may enter yourself and find nothing," I suggested, gesturing. "You will see that it is a miracle."

"You both think yourselves clever." He turned to me as he pulled a bejeweled dagger from his belt. "But I will chase him from his hiding place!"

King Thomas then closed and latched each door before attending the final open door before the throne. Holding the point of the dagger before him, he entered the box, thrusting out the weapon as he moved.

"Close the last door behind me so your magician cannot escape," he said. "Now Old James, avoid my blade if you have worthy arts to do so!"

When the king had fully entered the box I closed the last door as he'd commanded and dropped the final latch.

* * *

For many weeks the magician's box stood opened before the unoccupied throne waiting for its sovereign to reappear in the world. No other man, of course, dared to enter the box to search for his lost king, nor could any man decipher the mystery of his disappearance, except to say that the old magician's declaration had indeed proven true.

Eventually four soldiers moved the box from the great hall and let the clergy burn it as an evil omen on the land; the young prince soon returned from his sojourn with monks and assumed his father's bloody throne. Fortunately, the young man's mind knew nothing of Thomas' cruelty, and he even found it in his heart to forgive my inadvertent removal of his father from the world.

When the boy inquired of the manner of his father's dire fate, I only told him that the king wished to find the greatest magician in his lands, and unfortunately succeeded. King Thomas could not find the way to repudiate a master of the craft, and in attempting to do so, fell victim to the hazards of vanity.

I did not disclose to the young prince that I had found that magician first, and had paid him handsomely for a bravura performance of his art, not for the king, but for *myself*, which, all things in heaven and earth considered, concluded more entertainingly than I could have prayed for. Nor did I disclose the true fate of his father—for only the old magician knew which door reopened unto paradise, and which doors led on to the flames of perdition.

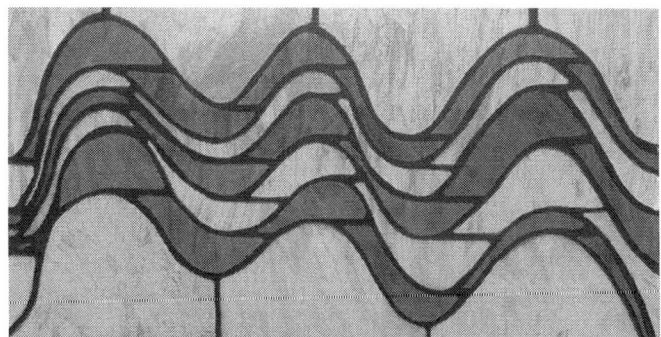

Flowing Ribbons, by Phillip Fitzsimmons

Seek Strength

by Ella Walsworth-Bell

When winter of your soul is long and dark--
days are short and weak sunshine filters through the office window:
life is central heating, electric blankets, tepid soup, dampness permeates into
the core of your being.

Listen to the singing of your heart.
Deep in the mountain, Ice-Smaug guards treasures beyond your wildest dreams.
Seek them. For there is a map chiselled into your flesh.
There is a path to the beach. Take it. You are yet unformed.

And as the dwarves of Moria follow the ore;
you shall find ranks of robe clad women on the shores of the ocean at dawn.
Consort with them.
Shed yourself of clothing.
Shiver as you gaze with copper-sharp eyes into the pewter pool of morning.

This may hurt.

Step closer to the frozen forges.
Wince as your shoe-soft feet are rasped by the sand.
Enter the ocean. This is your other world.
One where your calves will be slapped by steel cold waves,
where you will hear the crash and pound of hammer-grey sea on anvil rocks.
Energised by life's breakers

Only then, when you are fully immersed in glittering water
will you see that you
— yes, you —
are the raw rock of life.

And only by entering the molten ocean at dawn
can you run through the portal, be forged in this smithy.
You shall not form armour from this,
nor weapons. No blades of death,
no swords or daggers will ensue. This is no men's world.
And dwarves cannot be measured by the length of their beards.

No, as you stand on the sand,
with sunrise, you will stoop to the ground
there — glistening — perfectly formed —
will be your heart, fresh and clean and
> *yours, anew.*

An Ocean Away

by Adam Levine

Medusa watched the row boat depart from the vessel anchored off the west side of her Great Aunt Lydia's island. She had been tending to the garden but paused to follow the rowboat as it disappeared into the shadows created by the late afternoon sun beating down on the ship. Medusa was sure it was the neighboring villages delivering a tribute of slaughtered goats for the new moon which was already visible in the cloudless sky.

Her family had received the property through her Great Aunt Lydia's estate. Even though the property had been in the family for years, her family still referred to it as her Great Aunt's. Medusa was not even the last of her siblings to stay here. Her sister Euryale relaxed here when she was between careers. Medusa thought it would be a good place to stay out of the limelight for a while after the wedding.

The deliveries were perhaps a relic of her sister's time here. On each new moon, the villages would drop off the slaughtered goats at the rocky base of the trail that led up from the beach to the house. Medusa left the villagers a note after the first delivery. It was a very thoughtful card with lovely penmanship, requesting that the villagers, if they wouldn't mind, could first butcher the meat themselves, and deliver the prepared cuts of mutton instead. Medusa had a short-lived smile when she carried the meat wrapped in twine and butcher paper up the trail. The note omitted it was actually her sister who would fly over to the villages and eat them, while Medusa remained earthbound and had no intention of rowing anywhere.

Medusa could understand the villager's fear of her sister. Euryale had the wings, the bat nose, and the bear claws. When Medusa looked in a mirror with the snakes in her hair covered, she looked just like the villagers. These days, it was not clear that such an offering would even appease her sister as Euryale had recently become a pescatarian.

Medusa wished that she could give a note to the other visitors who seemed to arrive at the most inopportune times. Some would let their booming voices precede their arrival, bellowing their titles as champions from distant shores come to slay the gorgon for their betrothed. They traipsed around the island, their swords prophylactic in their scabbards, as if love's protection possessed the air. Others unsheathed their swords immediately, and the steel would shake in their hands as they covered the island searching for her.

She liked to hide, which generally worked. Most men would arrive on the island, search for a few hours, decide they had the wrong address, and depart. The ones that remained, she would try to lead outside, as close to the island cliffs as possible, where a strong wind might knock them off the island onto the rocks below.

When she gardened, she would stare at the statues that surrounded her. She liked to imagine that they would come up the path from the beach to find a beautiful maiden tending her garden instead of some monster frothing for a fight. In an instant, questioned if they arrived on the wrong island, whether here, so far from home, the vows to their betrothed still mattered. She convinced herself that their mouths were agape in that instance not from their own changing corporal form, but her beauty. It was only an added benefit that the statues these men turned into made great planters for tomatoes.

The house was becoming a mess. Once they turned to stone, they were far too heavy to drag after the fact. She could no longer enter through the front door or the patio off the kitchen. It required a dexterity that she never possessed just to enter. Still, it required that she knew that they were there.

She did not know why they turned to stone when they saw her, though she had a strong inkling it was the snakes that now made up the strands of her hair, continuously coiling and hissing in her ear. They were the only thing that had changed since the wedding. When she looked in the mirror herself, her head wrapped, it was as if the last year had never occurred.

Medusa wandered over from her garden to watch the boat's arrival. Birds that would rest in the island's trees started singing. The rower closed in on the rocks and hopped into the water. The water rose to his knees, as he pulled the boat towards the shore.

Medusa heard her phone ringing back at the house over the bird's call. She had left her phone in the living room, charging on the coffee table next to a puzzle. If the sound reached down to the shore, the man did not acknowledge it. The phone continued to ring. She wound up the garden path towards the sliding doors that opened into the living room. The statues did not block that entrance yet. She tried her best to keep the living room clean.

"Ducey." her sister Euryale said when Medusa put the phone to her ear.

"Yes."

"What do you think about Greige?"

"The monster at Thaumos's wedding? Mom kept coming around to point out all the single mortal monsters there, like after 25 years I'm not capable of figuring these things out myself. She thinks I'm still a child."

"She doesn't think that you are a child."

"Last Valentine's Day, did she send you a Valentine's Day card?"

"No, she sent my kids one. They were cute."

"That is what I mean. She sent me one."

"It doesn't mean anything. She just wants to see you settle down and be happy." The word 'settle' struck Medusa's ear through all the hissing as resignation. An admission that she wouldn't be able to experience the far reaches of love.

"She doesn't care what I think about them as long as they are mortal," Medusa responded to her sister. "Even logistically, when was I supposed to see him again, even if we hit it off? He lives oceans away."

"His name was Greg, but since you brought it up, what was wrong with him, his teeth too big?"

"He's only single because he ate his last wife."

"Mom said there was a man over the last time she called. She could hear him in the background. When Dad called it was the same thing. None of us understand why you think you are going to do any better than Poseidon. A daughter of a crab god and sea monster princess, and you just blow off Poseidon and decamp to Great Aunt Lydia's house."

"I told you Poseidon was never my boyfriend. We were never even dating."

"So that's what you're calling it these days? You and Poseidon were gone a long time."

"I was just washing off my dress. Thirteen goat sacrifices are too many."

"I guess you are the experts in how to honor the gods. But when you turn down Poseidon, it doesn't just look bad on you, it looks bad on our entire family. Then we hear through the grapevine that men are visiting you at all hours. Maybe we could say that you are more interested in them, but you blow them off, too."

"I've told you, they are trying to kill me."

"Have you tried the apps? There is Tinder, Bumble, Hinge, Island Hop, Monster Mash. When I was waiting to pick Gaea up at pre-school, Velia told me about another one that her brother is on, God Tier."

"I know all of them. I don't get any matches. I crop out the snakes and everything." She had tried everything, the French braids, Cretan knots, even cut her braids to shorten them but they still grew back as snakes.

"Have you tried putting them back in? Once I learned to love my bat nose is when I found my husband Cephacles."

Euryale was in a place where advice came easy. When she was staying at Great Aunt Lydia's island, Euryale watched a Netflix special about a former chiropractor who had adjusted herself into a new-age guru, which led to the purchase of the guru's book. One of the changes was to become a pescatarian. The book helped her get rid of the eczema that was making her skin so scaly. A few more changes to the way she looked on the inside with a positive mindset and she netted a new career and a husband. She was telling everyone she could about the book; she sent the book to Medusa for her eczema, but Medusa thought it was for relationship help. Medusa understood Euryale's excitement, just not her inability to take Medusa off email chains she forwarded each week about the guru's next 4-day conference.

"Yes, I even tried that. One of us has actually been single and had to use them." Medusa hoped her prospective matches had to view her in person and weren't turning to stone in front of a phone screen.

"You don't have to scream at me." Euryale had also learned this subtle mortal tactic of changing the subject from their mother.

"I'm not screaming," Medusa screamed at her sister.

"Anyway, greige is actually a color for the cabinets. It's like beige and grey together, works like a neutral. I think it would look nice with all those statues. Don't tell me that you haven't looked at the cabinet colors I sent you?"

"I haven't had the time. I don't think I'm going with greige."

"Why don't you have any interest in this? Mom and Dad should have had you make more decisions when we were younger. You should be grateful that we are doing this all for you."

Medusa did have a lack of interest in the construction of the home, save for it happening. Roman Numeral 1, Medusa just wanted space, she did not care how the wallpaper complimented the statues, or what light fixtures went above the kitchen table. Roman Numeral 2, she thought it might be best to leave the island anyway. It was apparent from the steady stream of visitors that her coordinates were known.

This all started when Medusa requested to knock down a few walls at her Great Aunt Lydia's house to give her a better view of her surroundings when she was home. A few weeks ago, she woke up in the middle of the night to get a glass of water from the kitchen. She had just shut off the lights in the kitchen and was about to walk back down the hallway to her bedroom when she nicked herself on the sword of a man who had just turned to stone. She barely even saw him coming around the corner. To her family, knocking down one wall evidenced a need for an open floor plan, which justified a new kitchen. A new kitchen required new cabinets. Euryale thought it would have value for potential renters anyway. In truth, her sister had an eye for interior design, though no one would be writing poetry about it. Still, her sister could envision the space: Medusa needed something tangible.

"Well, can you at least get a measurement for me? I forgot how big the island was." Euryale said.

"I'm not measuring the entire island."

"I mean the island in the kitchen."

Medusa thought she had left the measuring tape on the kitchen table. She walked down the hall, her feet cool against the terra cotta tiles to the kitchen. She adjusted herself around the statue she cut herself on a few weeks prior. When she turned into the kitchen she spied the man from the boat, his muscles clenched behind a bronze shield. She scampered back behind the statue. Medusa watched as the stranger torqued his body through statues and around the island with the farmhouse sink.

"Did you get it?" Medusa heard Euryale ask through the speaker. Medusa cupped the speaker on the phone. He didn't react but continued to push forward through the kitchen.

"Could you quiet down, a man is walking around my house."

"Who?"

"I don't know. I didn't invite him. I came inside to get the phone."

"I wonder who it could be? Let me think about it."

"Looks like Norman," Medusa said under her breath.

"Who's Norman? Is that one of the boys that has been coming over since you left Poseidon?"

He was not one of those boys. A few months after she had been on the island, a particularly violent storm passed through knocking down tree branches and decapitating some statues. When she walked outside to assess the damage, Medusa saw a man washed ashore on the beach. She did not know how he had arrived. She looked out to the ocean, its waters now calm. She scanned the beach, finding no evidence of a boat's destruction.

Her instinct was to wait. He had found himself on the island and if he needed he could find himself off. There was no reason to engage. For hours he lay there motionless. She did not know whether he was even alive. Then he began howling with such pain that it rooted in her and pulled her towards him. She wanted it to stop for him. She walked up beside him with a calmness that she was doing a kindness for a friend. She stood above him. His skin was tan from the sun, a crisp red where his shirt used to be, smooth like he was already polished stone. She waited a moment looking out into the ocean, a reprieve before his last breath. By staring down at him, it would be over for him. She felt his waterlogged fingers grip her calf.

"Help me," he said.

She looked down at him. He was looking right at her. She was staring right into his eyes. When her body registered that he had not turned, it pulsated as if the lightning from the night before would split her in two. She dug her heels into the sand to steady the vibrations in her body.

"Yes," she said.

She wanted to luxuriate in the waves of that feeling, but then she noticed the source of his pain: infected abrasions around his eyes. She took some herbs from the garden and mixed a paste she was taught would heal wounds. She spread it out on his face until he looked like a monster himself, still better than half the people she saw at Thamous's wedding. She wrapped his eyes in cloth. She brought him water. When he had enough strength, she helped him to his feet, and led him through a gauntlet of statues, through the house, and deposited him on the couch in the living room. He slept for the next three days.

When he awoke she was just happy to have him there. She had been alone for so long that she found that she had almost forgotten the joy in her voice until he commented that it was relaxing.

First, it was just normal stuff, name, where from, which school, siblings, dogs or cats. She would constantly remind him, as if reminding herself, to turn away when removing the bandages each day while redressing the wounds. While he slept, she had watched televisions shows, but she wasn't going to watch them with him and have to explain everything that was happening. They would listen to the radio.

A man called into the station requesting a song for his wife. The DJ recognized the voice of the caller, and the caller confirmed he indeed dialed in the day before with the same request. Norman didn't understand why the man didn't just buy the record. Medusa thought it was sweet that he was requesting a song that his love could hear an ocean away. Still, they listened together and in this way, the caller's song became their song.

As he recovered, she would take him around the garden and describe the statues. He always thought they were from a different kingdom than she said. She thought that he was doing it just to incense her since he would compliment her on how life-like they felt to the touch. The snakes were beginning to develop into split ends.

She found herself looking forward to an evening cocktail. She was adjusting to the company. She poured drinks with a nervous hand. She hit his glass to cheers, and the carbonation bubbled up over the ridge of his glass and drenched his hand. She brought him a towel to dry his hands, and while drying them, their hands, first, and then their bodies intertwined.

Then one day, while making drinks in the kitchen, she heard the radio playing and walked into the living room to find Norman up next to the stereo with a phone to his ear. The DJ comes on the radio and Norman requests a song, their song.

" For a girl an ocean away." He says. Even through the bandages, she could feel the heat of his stare. He removed the bandages in a circular motion around his head as the song began to play. Medusa moved forward to clutch his body. She tried to avert her gaze by placing her head on his chest. They swayed on the carpet, wrapped in each other's arms. But now that he was stronger, she was no match for his desire. She had to look at him, she couldn't stay here forever. The song had to end.

She turned her gaze from his chest and met his eyes. She was able to look into his soft blue irises. Due to her nursing, she had cleared up his issues. She is staring into his eyes when one of the last remaining snakes breaks free of its braids when he is about to speak.

" You are". . . He is petrified and starts falling on top of her. Medusa spins from under his armpit as he crashes onto the floor of the living room.

"No, it is not one of those boys." She said still not believing she had said his name so casually.

"Is he trying to kill you, too?" Euryale joked. "I swear they are trying to kill us all. Cephacles is going to grind me down. All I ask him to do is wash the dishes, and he doesn't even do that. Then just put the dish towel in the washing machine, and I get home from taking our children to piano lessons and what do I find on top of the dirty laundry, but the dish towel? Are you going to say hello?"

"Wouldn't it be easier if I let him wander through the house? I can hide talking to you and eventually, he'll come to realize I'm not here and leave."

"Go and say hello, what an excuse."

"He's trying to kill me."

"It is always an issue with you."

"What's he look like?"

Medusa found it difficult to describe the man to her sister. The parts of his body that she was noticing, she didn't want to tell her sister. Euryale had made fun of her for days for just having a friend with a name that sounded like male anatomy. Still, even the most threadbare description was enough.

"Oh, I remember now." Euryale said, "When I was dropping off Gaea at piano class, I ran into Despoina and she told me that Perseus is on a hero's quest. It is quite sweet if I remember it correctly. Perseus forgets a wedding gift, so he offers the king anything he desires. Can you imagine how he would treat his woman? He's single too. You have to go meet him. You are living a myth if you think Poseidon is coming back. Can't complain to me about the opportunities that come with living on an island and then a man, a man like Perseus, comes to your door. You act like a blind man is just going to wash up on shore. What are you going to wear? "

"I have that green jumper that I wore to---I'm not going." She corrected herself. "I'll just let him come and go."

"What are you going to do with your hair? I would hate to see you cover it all up. Have you watched *Queen's Gambit* yet? She wears the cutest head-scarves; you never see that anymore."

"Ok, ok, but I have to go get ready."

"Ducey," her sister said, "please do this. I have to go."

Her sister hung up. Medusa went back to her room. She went into her closet, picked out the green jumper, and wrapped a silk hair wrap tight around her head. She gave herself one last look in the mirror. It had been so long since she put herself out there. She felt like a winged horse was beating its hooves inside her. She strode out to meet her destiny. The snakes' hisses muffled as they suffocated in the cloth.

To the Red Beacons
by Nicole Ai

In grand waves shivers sail — away from the earth.
The edge where briny voices are the crests, ride
at my reflection. Anchors, sharp ritual of the wavering night.

I face an inscrutable vision: plumes of fire ruffled by their watery rhythms—
Or is it now a waking dream that sobs beneath crimson swamps?
The visions are always figments,
water-bodies and mothers
directing mud over my untidy skin.

If the sensations (breathing in and out in two short spaces)
     are what I find serene, I am yet to convict,
to be derided by the polar grace ahead.
As the celestial forces in the sky

draw back with fear inside their sphere,
those febrile solstices are desperate on butterfly's spirals
when their effulgent wings are pinched on walls
under the pale moonlight.

Now here, the silence awaits. How secluded, a drained hermit in
worldly dust under her lotus feet, red beacons are too hot for the earth. Dance!
      They
           lost
                utterly ———— unstable,
sacrificing their lustrous hues atop each thunderous climax
of fleeting waves, weighing the years but abnormally lively.
A fist twists its darkish veins, effusively signaling

the taps within a nymphal heart after hundreds of times when a body rot
in terrible silence, in the inner sea of desolated lands.
The distraction of solitude, however,
never jades the mirror of my face, and only greets me passionately.
Such red-blooded, such unbending, watery feathers,
when was the last time this animalistic apparition ascended?
Eyes to eyes,
they mottle the waves, reincarnating in their warm, ripening souls.

But the red beacons remain timeless. The mother laughs,
quivering against the daylight during its beckoning march:
You are ridiculously frail...
                You cannot rope the will.
                          You cannot ride the colour!
For a reflection
      that sees her body as a bind, she is vowing the most miraculous thing
in horrible solitude and blazing through the abyss between
two glows, equally merry
amidst the presence of the wonderful Divine.

The Reluctant Monk: A Mythopoeic Version

by Andoni Cossio

Oh, yes, I remember well the shiny cuirass that swept me off my feet, part of an armor that later became rusted and dented, to finally rest on a perch. It was sold in the end to fund my husband's disturbing drinking habit. Reality hit me hard and often my husband, too. Soon enough I found myself doing all the chores without servants, while I realized my dowry was diminishing by the day. As a wealthy orphan, I could have well become a nun. My life would have been better, and I would not have to take care of an abusive and lazy rascal whose temple was the tavern and whose mistress was the wine flagon. I told him I could not bear this marriage anymore and he replied: "bear it you must, for the law says so." I had to find a way to unmarry before he beat me to death or he drunk us both to destitution.

My husband's life may seem worthless, but he held it dearer than his beloved wine and had a pathological fear of death. At the slightest sign of failing health, he thought he foresaw his own demise and threw a most horrible tantrum until the illness waned. Only in these occasions, he prayed to the divinities and swore he would reform himself.

With this in mind, I made the most of the occult lore I had been secretly learning for years, and I prepared a beverage that made the drinker experience complete body paralysis while retaining sight, hearing and speech. The wits become clouded and the vision blurs, and if it is concocted with alcohol the experience deftly resembles near-death. A tasteless potion combined with wine, a drink my husband felt naturally inclined towards, was the perfect mix. When that night he asked me to uncask a new barrel, my plan was already in motion.

It did not take him long to be so intoxicated and under the influence of the beverage that he had to lie in bed, the room spinning around him and the paralysis taking effect. When I heard him scream that he could not move, I proceeded to enchant my voice with a charm to make it deeper and more otherworldly. I then disguised myself with an ample hooded robe and wore a mask of the Soul Collector, that I had purposefully crafted.

"Alfred, Alfred!" I vocalized with care and at a slow pace, dragging and distorting each syllable. I had never seen my husband so scared since a night two years ago when he had severe food poison. Beads of sweat broke out on his brow.

"Go to hell, wife! And chuck aside that robe, and go call a healer, please, I can't move!" Alfred's voice trembled and he whined when uttering the word 'please.' I had not been addressed courteously since the day of our wedding; this was working.

"No healer can cure you, I'm not your wife, and YOU are soon joining my menagerie of wrong-making souls."

"What? What do you mean? Who are you? Please stop, I haven't done anything wrong, I just like wine a bit too much, please forget my wrongs, will you? I'll be good from tomorrow on, I'll even moderate my drinking."

I saw that my plan was working and I proceeded with it. I raised my voice and distorted it further to sound more menacing:

"Not nearly enough! I am here to take you by force from your flesh and bones! You will join my hoard of wrongdoers; I want a new pet to play with. No matter what you promise, you are coming with me!"

The Soul Collector was a well-known legend in our region, and one way too fearsome to disregard by someone as scared of death as Alfred. He panicked at the thought of enduring an eternal sentence for his crimes.

"No, please! I beg for mercy! Let me live, I'll do whatever you say without complaint!" Alfred stuttered with agony on every word.

"Uh, a repenting soul? That is not so appealing. I only let loose those that go about without causing harm to anyone or anything. Are you truly willing to mend your ways?"

"Yes, if that'll save me, your wish is my command," he uttered mustering all the courage he had left.

"All right," I said slowly. "There is a way that can make up for your behavior for all these years. A radical change."

"A radical change! How radical?

"This is your last chance, Alfred."

"I'm so sorry, I won't hesitate, I promise!"

"Fine, Alfred. Trick me and you will feel my grip on your neck. Tomorrow, as soon as the rooster wakes and sings, you will head towards the closest abbey; do not even say goodbye to your wife. You will relinquish all your possessions and become a faithful monk for the rest of your days. Inebriate yourself or hit someone once again and I will pay you a final visit."

"Will do, will do!" he wailed. "I want to keep breathing a little longer."

"As a reminder of your promise, I'll leave the habit you will wear from tomorrow onwards on the chest at the foot of your bed. Bye, for a few hours or forever. You decide."

Alfred fell into uneasy sleep until the fowls announced the coming of a new day. By then the effects of the drink had vanished. When he noticed the habit that I had procured from the local order to make my case more convincing, he was horrified. This was no nightmare; he had no time to lose. Without hesitation, my husband headed straight for the neighboring abbey lest the Soul Collector should make another sudden appearance.

Some days after, the plan was an absolute success: Once Alfred renounced all his earthly possessions, I was the sole inheritor, and I was able to live in peace and quiet without worries for many moons. Alfred found greater happiness, too. I soon learnt that he recovered from his alcoholism, found a new purpose in life within the religious community, and even fell deeply in love with copying and glossing manuscripts!

After this miracle, I realized that there is no greater power in my world than living myths. Is that so in yours?

How the Moons Came to Be
by Mary Johnson

When time began, the twins, Anan and Senen, played in the void. And he was beauty, and she was grace. And he was laughter, and she was song. Where Anan led, Senen followed; where Senen led, Anan followed. So the holy twins danced and sang the world into being. When one sang, the other dreamed. When one dreamed, the other sang. And what both dreamed together came to be.

So they dreamed the sun, the stars, and the earth under their feet. So they dreamed the rivers and mountains and the sea. And Senen and Anan took stone and earth and made balls. They each made one, and they played ball together.

This is how they played. They threw the balls to each other and caught them. And at each catch, they stepped backward so that the throw would be longer. They played across the White Mountains, and all the three rivers, and the gulf of Esa. They sang as they played, and the grasses and flowers began to grow under their feet.

Then Senen threw his ball so far that it went up into the sky and stayed there.

"Bring it down again, brother!" Anan said to him. Senen leaped to the top of Mount Enea and reached as high as he could. But he could not touch his ball of stone and earth. Then Senen wept, for he was a young god, and he had never known loss before.

Anan embraced him. Then she said, "Look! How beautiful your ball is, up there in the sky. I will throw mine, too." She threw her ball as high as she could, so that it, too, stayed in the sky. But she did not throw as high as Senen, so her ball stayed closer to the earth. It became the great moon that the invaders call Thonn. But we know it as Ala, the love between a brother and sister. And Senen's ball is the lesser moon, and its name is Nen, the joy in the play of children. For the holy twins were very young when the world was new.

So the moons stayed in the sky and gave light to the night. And Anan and Senen still dance and sing throughout the heavens and the earth. They are in the silence before the word, and in the thought before the deed. And when we speak out of the silence that is love, we honor them. And when we act out of the thought that is joy, we honor them. And may we always honor them.

That is all.

ALL IN
A Loki and Sigyn Tale

by Danielle Krikorian

Drip. Drop. Drip. Drop.

In a dim cavern of gray and cold, where frozen stalagmites also drip down, I do not dare look at my husband's face. But I know for some time now, his gaze has always been turned upward and wide-eyed, although he can barely see the bottom of the bowl collecting the venom that drizzles in drips and drops.

Drip. Drop. Drip. Drop.

My love refuses to look at me. He doesn't speak to me. Not anymore. Not even when he knows my relentless, lovelorn heart still stays with him. He does little to care for it. I should know, for I am Sigyn, his wife. I *was* once his love.

Loki murmurs weak charms that have grown hollow. Sometimes, he strains against the chains, made from the guts of our son, that bind him. He knows it's useless, but that never stopped the Trickster before, and it certainly won't stop the god now.

What a god he was: exiled or homebound, prisoner or free, his mischief knew no bounds. Again, I should know. I've seen it. I've played as a pawn in it. Yet, I'd do it again even if I knew it would lead me to where I am now, on my knees, shielding my husband in the best way I could, even if it was meager help. I will strive to comfort him until that day of Ragnarök when the end comes for all of us gods, even tricksters.

Drip. Drop. Drip. Drop.

There are many things I could say to my love as the iridescent venom continues to slide down two ivory fangs from Skaði's large, pale, and copper-scaled snake, rippling the pool with its drips and drops, echoing in the dim cavern, too loud for a loyal, lovelorn heart like mine to bear. A reminder of all that he has done and all that he is.

Loyal. That's what I am. That's what I've been called. The Æsir told me, "Never has there been a being so loyal as Sigyn."

I had replied, "It's better than the lot of all of you who jump from side to side for whatever benefits you. What is life if we have nothing to commit ourselves to? Even an immortal life is worthless without devotion to something or someone."

"If your unwavering loyalty is to as mischievous husband as Loki, then you are a fool, too."

A fool. I've been called that before in my godly life for the feeble attempts and wasted pursuits of trying to get my own way in the Nine Realms. It never led me anywhere except to become the wife of the God of Mischief. Perhaps that is what they meant.

I refuse to be a fool. I am loyal, and loyalty is a trait most admirable, which is always what I wanted to be. Yet the words of the Æsir have left imprints and impressions on my mind. Am I a fool? Is it truly foolishness that guides me? Could I actually be both loyal and a fool?

Drip. Drop. Drip. Drop.

    Loki's muffled moan against his chains threads into my focus, unweaving the musings that were tangling with the thorny feelings piercing my heart. I steal a glance at my handsome husband, pale as the crescent moon, the red of fire swept into long, straight locks of hair. It was Loki's eyes, which lit up when he was most excessively diverted, that I liked most about his countenance. I liked his slender, strong, muscular body and his lithe limbs, too. The very ones that tangled with mine when he made love to me. When he loved me.

    How he loved me is a phenomenon I will certainly never forget. Our shared love began when we first met. Cliché as it was, I fell for him at first sight, although I had previously heard of his mischievous ventures. Those ventures interested me—a prelude to when I finally saw him.

    It was in Odin's palace in Asgard. A great hunt guided by Skaði led to the excuse for feasting. The tapestries on the walls were all aglow beside the torches blazing with honey-bright fire, showing symbols of all the deities, most of whom were gathered around the fire in the center of the room. I was standing near the back, by a braided, wooden column, trying my best to converse and look serenely confident, although banquets made me want to retreat to somewhere I felt I had power. Among the Æsir, I had little.

    Loki did not see me at first. He was in the crowd of the Æsir and other minor gods and goddesses. He was tapping his fingers on the broad shoulder of Idun, who was wearing a fleece cloak made of golden wool, her russet brown hair loosely braided with pale golden apple blossoms and vines that held her tresses together. Idun tried her best to ignore the tapping, knowing very well who was at fault. Loki had played this small trick on her dozens of times, so I've been told, and Idun had no patience for him. Therefore, she looked in the opposite direction, expecting to find the Trickster and chastise him for his annoyance. She did not find him. Instead, he was on the side from which he was tapping her shoulder. When Idun finally turned to find him, Loki poked her in the nose. Idun flinched, flicking him away as one does to an irritating insect. Loki chuckled snarkily, then turned in my direction.

    He saw me, and his eyes lit up. They shone, diverted, bright, and almost blinding. His languid smile went a tad slack, but he straightened his shoulders. I gazed back at him, my breath catching in my throat, wiggling like a nervous fish caught in a net. I tried to play coy for the rest of the feast that night. I avoided him, although every part of me wanted to be near him. I did not want him to think that I was desperate for the affection that the other gods and goddesses lacked in giving, except for my teacher, Baldur, who saw how my eyes could not help but look for the Trickster.

    Baldur was the best of the pantheon—the gentlest. From him, I learned what it was like to be merciful when I was often left out on my own, harboring grudges until they festered like boils branched out like thorny weeds in my heart. As I watched how Baldur acted with each and every flawed deity, it inspired me, and I let go. I cleaned my wounds and pulled up those weeds and roots, and I began to thrive, not caring so much anymore; that was when more of the gods took notice of me, although it did bother me that they considered me foolish. Still, they gave me the title of mercy. Loyalty followed later, after Loki and I became involved.

    When Baldur caught my traveling gaze, he frowned and slowly shook his head—a warning. One that I did not heed. Even Baldur's good nature and forgiveness seemed to have its limits. Time would tell if mine had any.

    I think Loki must have been impatiently waiting for me to speak to him. However, his impatience reached its limit and he approached me. He said nothing, so I obliged him.

    "I've heard of you, Trickster."

    "Good things, I hope." A twinkle in his dark green eyes made me blush.

    "Is mischief ever good?"

"If you know how to wield it properly."

"Teach me."

"Oh, I don't know, Sigyn."

"You know my name?" My breath seemed to be slowly taken from me.

"Truly. I, too, have heard of you. You seem too *merciful* for mischief-making."

At that, I grew bold. Taking a step closer to him, I whispered into his elf-like ear, "Try me. I'm all in."

After that, the rest was history. We lay awake together, watching the green, yellow, pink, and violet lights waver in the sky like rivers as the stars battled to have their share and shine in the night sky. The sight reminded me of Loki's diverted eyes, which closed when he kissed me, deep, long, hard. They stayed closed as he dreamt of causing more treasured trouble in my arms.

Loki, the treasure of my arms.

The day before our wedding, he told me, "There is nowhere I would rather be than in your arms. Well, that and making mischief with you."

However true that was, Loki could never be truly tied down, even in his love for me. He had affairs in which he produced Odin's eight-legged horse, a goddess of the dead, the World Snake, and Fenrir the Wolf. I did my best to ignore this infidelity. I must have succeeded, given that I stayed with him, adventuring, making love under those lights in the northern night sky, and playing tricks.

That is one thing the tales that mortals have written about the gods have not made clear: that I helped in Loki's wild adventures in the Nine Realms. I was the one who cut Sif's golden braids as she slept. It was my own fingers that stole Freyja's necklace. I cheated some dwarves in order for my husband to keep chaos strung around the Realms. I told Loki to test me. I may be the most merciful of the pantheon, but that doesn't mean I can't have my fun. It gives me something and someone to have mercy for.

"You know, you don't have to do this, Sigyn." He spoke for the first time in what has seemed like ages. Maybe it has been ages, and it rattles the memories in my mind until they shatter like shards of ice, melting in the heat of the moment.

I'm staring at his deceitful lips, not knowing whether he actually spoke or if I imagined it. But slowly, he lowers his gaze until his undiverted eyes, glazed with healing haze, are level with mine. I wonder how clearly he can see me. My heart beats emphatically to the rhythm of a war drum.

"You don't have to do this," he repeats.

I swallow as the sound of his honeyed voice edged with bitterness sends frightened excitement up my back; the very back he pressed his large hands with long, slender fingers against when he pulled me in for an embrace. Or perhaps it's anticipation for a battle of words, and my back straightens.

"I want to," is all I can muster.

"I know." He smirks.

"Do you not want me to?"

Loki tries to shrug, but he can barely do so with his arms pulled back so tightly. "It's better than being poisoned, which I am from time to time."

He references when the bowl I use as his shield gets too full, and I have to leave him momentarily defenseless against the drip drops of venom to pour the collection out. When the venom does manage to reach him, it seeps into his eyes, making him shudder and ache with such ferocity that the whole cavern shakes. Sometimes, I think the Earth does, too.

At his remark, my arms, which have tirelessly been raised up, holding the bowl, finally feel an ache that has been long since numbed from the first day of his punishment. They grow so weak that they threaten to pull themselves close to my chest.

Drip. Drop. Drip. Drop.

"Don't stop now," Loki says, eyes slightly wider.

I force my arms to rise straighter and higher. "I'm not."

"I know."

"Then why did it seem like you were giving me a choice?"

He pauses. "Because you've longed and lingered after me forever. I thought you would have tried to move forward with your life before Ragnarök begins."

"Which will be soon?"

"I cannot tell." The corner of his mouth lifts in a sly smile.

Frowning, I let the pull of gravity tug at my chin. My lashes fall over my eyes. "Perhaps it would be best for the End of the World to begin. My world ended a long time ago."

"No, Sigyn. Your world just stopped turning."

My head snaps back up to look at him. Jaw clenching, I reply, "You made it stop." He cocks his head, causing some of his long fire-red hair to fall over his shoulder. "You were—are my world. So it stopped when you did."

"Because of you," he replies.

Breath catching in my throat, it threatens to burst my chest from the inside out. I know exactly what he means—the one time I failed him. The one time my loyalty failed him.

The prelude began when the gods, mainly Idun, said to me, "You'd be better off without your disloyal husband, Sigyn. I know your loyalty is stuck to him like tree sap. But that's what you are the longer you stay with him. I know you have your fun with him in the Realms and in your bed. But haven't you wondered what you would be like if you were free to live your own eternal life?"

"Nothing would ever be the same again," I replied."

Idun nodded. As she passed by me, her scent leaving behind a trail of apple blossoms and gold dust, she left me with a lingering thought, a hopeful fantasy. "You may find another man to love that can do something more that Loki cannot do: return the loyalty that you give."

Those worlds toiled within me, making my nerves wrack and my imagination stumble toward a hopeful light. Yes, it was true. I loved my husband and had the most pleasurable times with him. But when I heard of his affairs with other women, it left a sore ache in my heart that nothing, not even Time, the balm of all wounds, could heal. Perhaps it was because these liaisons kept happening.

Then, in the midst of winter, Loki guided a spear ironed with fatal mistletoe to peg good Baldur in the heart. I was stricken with grief. When Baldur dropped dead, the Æsir and other gods gathered in Aegir's hall. Loki, either drunk with ale or intoxicated with wickedness that was beyond mischief, began to slander and insult them. He mocked Bragi. He rumored that Freyja committed incest. He teased the one-handed Tyr. He poked fun at Odin. Loki then took on the rough Thor and his wife, in the Trickster's words, the "not so blameless" Sif. Loki went on and on until they threw him out.

"Sigyn, come!" he bid me. "My days in Asgard are coming to an end. Come!" He stretched out his hand to me, the wind howling as the snowfall made love with it.

Standing frozen, I did not take a single step toward him as I did when we first conversed. He killed my teacher, robbing Asgard and the rest of the Nine Realms of true purity and goodness. How could I go with him now? And could I leave the only home I ever knew? Could I leave on such a bitter note? Then I thought of Idun's weaving words. If I went with Loki, what would become of me when my husband goes on unfaithful ventures? Who would I turn to for comfort?

My reservations were riddled with anxiety. My hesitations grew heavy over us.

Loki's once bright eyes dimmed. His red hair was the only fiery thing in the icy world around us, under the horn-topped mountains and the dark woods beckoning for lost souls.

My husband's hand, which was always outstretched for me, retracted close to his chest when my hand wouldn't reach back. "You won't come, will you?"

Tears burning over my eyes and freezing down my cheeks, I said, "How can I now?"

Loki took several slow, shaky steps backward, then disappeared as the flurry took over.

I left him to a fate I knew he wasn't going to escape. However, I knew I would be there for him in the end.

Loki hid in the valleys. I knew this because that was a secret, he told me, of his love for them and the enchantment that befell the land where mountain bottoms collided. I kept his secret and let the Æsir find him in their own time. They would, eventually. Ragnarök was inevitable, as the prophecies foretold.

I continued my life looking after our empty home, taking care of the mortals who looked up to me, comforting them in their own troubles, although mine made me almost incapable of working. But my imagination and hope were infiltrated by Idun's words, still, and I tried to live the life I might have had away from my husband. I began to believe I could live a rewarding life without Loki.

Loki left his enchanted valleys only once. He appeared to me at night while I slept.

"Sigyn, wake up."

Eyes fluttering open, the moment I saw his red hair and dark eyes alight with hope, I began to weep.

"Sigyn, please come with me."

How badly I wanted to, but I could only cry and shake my head. "I can't! My love, I cannot go with you." I felt that I'd be discarding a bright future that the other gods convinced me I'd be gaining. I believed I'd disappoint the ones who looked after me. I also had bitterness tracing the edges of my heart because of my husband's attack on my teacher, Baldur.

His hopeful face became crestfallen. Then he disappeared to the valleys again, where the days spread thin like butter over bread into anticipating months. The Æsir could still not track the Trickster down. That was when I was walking with Idun, crying on her golden wool-cloaked shoulder, and Skaði and Heimdall, known as the Watchman. We walked through the emerald hills laced with snowdrops and crossed paths with Angrboda, the giantess who was the mother of three of Loki's children. Although we saw her from afar, it struck me she had some resemblance to me. Her hair, although darker than mine, was long and wavy, with few braids in it. She had the same oval-shaped face and small nose but dark eyes.

"You see it, too," Idun said.

"That she bears some of my features? Yes."

"But you're more beautiful, Sigyn. She's only the troll version of you," said Skaði, trying her best at comfort.

I turn to Heimdall. "Does Loki still go to her?"

Heimdall's gold and all-seeing eyes darken. "Do you truly want the Truth, Sigyn?"

"Truth sets you free. It lets you go."

"As you have not done for yourself." Idun was blunt.

My eyes plead with Heimdall's. I know the Truth, but my hope wants it to be false.

As more tears fill my eyes, the Watchman says, "I've seen what you don't want to." Confirmation.

"You must move on from the Trickster," Idun insisted. "He has moved on from you."

Heimdall said, "Has he? If he has affairs with the giantess, perhaps he does so because she somewhat resembles his loyal wife."

That gave me hope in my husband's love for me. Yet there would be no hope for Loki, although the end for him had still not come. But I will come for him once the end does.

34

Then, the time came for me to do so. The Æsir found that Loki had turned himself into a salmon, pink and crested with thunder-cloud gray, that slipped through the waters, skidded over the stony river ground, and slid between jagged rocks. His attempt was folly, for his undoing was sealed when he landed in a net of his own making.

And so his punishment was carried out. I came to see it, although my husband would not look at me. We both watched our son, Vali, be cursed into a wolf, tearing our other son, Narvi, from limb to limb before running off. The gods, cruel and hungry for revenge, took the guts and entrails of Narvi, fastened them around Loki, making them into iron-like chains, and bound him to the rocks of a stalagmite cave. Skaði placed a patient snake above my husband, its mouth forever widened, flashing ivory fangs that dripped with aching poison into Loki's eyes. When the gods left Loki to suffer, I knelt beside him, arms raised with a bowl to catch the poison to give him some comfort. It's the only thing I can control in regard to my trickster husband. Also, it serves as a punishment for me that I should still stay beside him, letting my knees ache against the cold stone floor, and my body stiffen and become numb as I shield him. So, I stayed with him.

Drip. Drop. Drip. Drop.

Loki then says, "The Æsir may still consider your loyalty to shine as they see you here now. But to me, it has dimmed. I tried to give it to you, the choice to redeem it. But you chose not to."

"I wanted to!" I screech. "You cannot fathom how much I wanted to." I shake my head, causing my hair to rustle and sway against my burgundy-red cloak. But I was persuaded to lead my life on my own."

"And now you've changed your mind? Is that why you stay with me? You're too late." He gives me one last harsh look and then closes his hazy eyes. The muscles in his jaw grow taut. All his body is tense underneath his black and emerald tunic, tied with a belt, riddled with cords strung with both metal and wooden beads.

I keep talking. "No, I haven't changed my mind. Not exactly. There are times I do regret letting you go. But I understand that you're not good for me, Loki. Despite that, my heart is forever tethered to you. It always will be. I still love you, even if you have moved on from me."

Loki opens his bright eyes, however hazy they were before, and they shine with a viciousness that only comes when he means harsh business.

"You'd burn with every drop of poison that befalls you," I continue. "Perhaps you should reconsider setting me free to move on."

"Truth is, Sigyn, you moved on when you made those choices."

My lips part, barely sucking in the shallowest of breaths. My heart pounds more fiercely than ever, trying to break free of its godly, boned cage. I only raise my arms higher.

Drip. Drop. Drip. Drop.

A drop of the iridescent poison slides down the edge of the bowl. The limit has been reached. Loki can sense it, too. I'll have to walk away to pour the poison into the foul basin at the edge of the cavern.

Loki watches me hesitate. He senses the question I now ask myself: Is it time to truly let go of him? I've held on for so long.
That's what I do best. I'll continue to do so.
And the cycle continues.

Slowly, I rise to my feet, the bowl quaking in my unsteady hands.

Drip. Drop. Drip. Drop.

The drops slide over the wooden bowl, overflowing. I turn to leave. Loki screams in agony as the drips and drops fall into his eyes. The sound is deafening. The ground beneath me shakes so violently that I lose my footing and stumble. Sharp stalagmites shatter around me. Hitting the ground with a hard thud, my arms become outstretched, and my hands lose their hold of the overfilled bowl. It falls far from me, splashing and sloshing its contents. The ground hisses and boils under the strength of the poison. Loki is still screaming; the ground is still quaking.

I curl up, my knees hitting my chin. My eyes are squeezed shut, waiting for a stalagmite to impale me. My heart is shivering, beating beyond control. I want to scream, but my voice is strangled, bottled up in my chest. It seems to last a godly lifetime.

The shivers and beats don't stop even when I realize the ground has become still and everything is quiet. Uncurling myself, I sit up and find Skaði's snake slithering away and Loki gone, unbound.

I knew I'd be here for Ragnarök to begin. I just hoped that Loki would have mercy on me and take me with him for one last adventure. It was foolish of me to hope that his forgiveness towards me was still possible.

I am both of what the gods said I was. I am a fool for staying by his side. I am loyal to him as he begins our world's end.

mushroom people
by Eleanor Farrell

In the light of the moon of the spring equinox
the shy mushroom people emerge from their rocks.
They've slumbered and dreamed through the long winter cold
Creating the stories that now can be told.

Some tales they are merry, while others are grim;
the choice of the teller is up to her whim.
Some tell of the death caps, who creep in the night
and shaggy mane armies so ready to fight.

And some of the stories are full of romance,
of fairy ring pairings and love of the dance.
A gallant young velvet foot spins in a whirl
and gifts a small oyster a spore like a pearl.

The celebrants dance while the moon is on high,
Their angel's wings fanning their joy to the sky.
And last, the old man of the woods will appear
to hallow the revels and hale the new year.

You Mustn't Disquiet the Fauna

by Jared Bentley

The Spring months in the Valley of Eden are to die for. When the first warm March sunrise crests the Blue Ridge Mountains, everything melts. Just as animals come out of their shallow shelters to frolic and forage, people too leave behind the warmth of their hearths to commune with nature.

The people of the Valley of Eden find peace and relaxation away from the bothers and burdens of modern society. The hum of industry and the buzz of passing cars quiet to nearly a whisper while nature's languages grow louder. One may hear them in the early morning or late, late at night—the chattering quarrels of squirrels, the winged songs of crickets, and the longing mating calls of robins, to name a few.

During the Spring months, many children are conceived. Few are delivered.

Yet one mother's water broke on Spring's first day, sending a runoff down her leg and onto the hardwood floor. She sought no doctors or hospitals but a steel drum bathtub and the neighbor across the valley who was one-quarter Shawnee.

That was the day Adam emerged into the world. He was born in Blue Ridge Mountain well water. His mother briefly eased her shoulders, having thought the end of it. But the contractions returned, and Eve was born shortly thereafter.

Their mother kissed them each on the forehead and bathed them in the bloody bathwater before consuming her placenta.

* * *

"We should never leave the Valley of Eden," Mother cried out to her congregation of twenty-seven women, fifteen men, and thirty children. Adam and Eve were among them, sitting in the first pew. "For it provides us with everything we need!"

The church roof was made of straw, held together by rounded wood beams. Adam liked to admire the wood that had been cleanly shaven of bark. Each beam had once been a tree. Each tree had once been in the forest. He wondered if he could change like the trees had. First, he'd have to abandon his roots.

"The forest gives and gives," Mother continued.

Adam often gazed upward while Mother spoke to all her *children*. He didn't bother listening to Mother's sermon. He had listened less and less since she'd told him half a year ago, "You only get a fever when you lie."

Adam knew that couldn't be true, since baby Ben had a fever at the end of summer and babies can't lie.

Instead of listening to Mother, he wondered what was outside the valley, whether he could ever visit Gatlinburg or Pigeon Forge. The towns were full of blasphemers, Mother had said.

Mother's footsteps drew closer, but Adam didn't heed their warning. He wondered what it might feel like to ride in a car or to use a computer. Mother's footsteps ceased and Adam heard a loud whack.

Pain shot through his hand and up his arm. Through welling tears, he saw the carved stick vanish up Mother's long-hanging sleeve. Beside him, Eve suppressed a giggle with her hand.

"Thank you all for listening." Mother shot a glare at Adam. "We will resume tomorrow morning. God bless our valley of Eden and remember..." Mother paused as the congregation said their mantra as one unit. "You mustn't disquiet the fauna."

* * *

Adam didn't care for prophecies, warnings, or rules. He cared about running. And he ran everywhere—through the valley of Eden, through the forest, along the river, and sometimes, even up the mountains—with his sister, Eve, always at his heels. Any time they were still, she would constantly pester him. Adam supposed that's why he rarely stopped running.

When his lungs tired, the two of them slowed and sat in the middle of a forest clearing. Adam was unsure if he had ever been to the clearing. The forest knew that he had not.

A slow-moving, narrow creek ran beside the clearing, an avenue for mountain runoff. It grew larger and larger fed by other tributaries the further down the valley it ran, until its mouth opened into the Lake of Gabriel. Adam knew these things, as sure as he knew the Earth was round. He felt it in the way he traversed the ground. He saw it in the sky. A flat earth was just another of Mother's lies. He wondered how many lies she had told in her life. He wondered what else might be a lie.

The two sat facing the river, grasping at their breath like it was running away from them. Eve tapped Adam's shoulder and motioned at something. "Look," his sister said, panting.

A peach tree gleamed in the midday sun.

Peaches were abundant in the valley of Eden but neither of them had seen fruit so ripe. The dew on their soft skin glittered in the silken rays cast down through the canopy. Each new peach they eyed was more beautiful than the last. Their color was a sunset.

"I dare you to eat one," Eve said. Adam could hear the thickness of salivation in her voice.

"I will if you do," Adam said.

The two children approached the tree in their hunger and thirst. With each step closer, they could nearly taste the peaches. They were only footsteps away when a snake exited from a nearby bush. The snake was striped black and red, the deadly colors cascading down its long, thin frame. It hissed and slithered before the tree as if coming to its defense.

The two children retreated. "You mustn't disquiet the fauna," Eve stated. But Eve had always been of two minds. She could believe something one day and disbelieve it the next, only to preach it a week later. It came as no surprise to Adam that as Eve recanted Mother's warning, she broke a small branch off of a nearby tree, and handed it to him.

Simply giving him the stick was enough to make him act. Adam stepped forward and with anger in his heart, he struck the snake just as Mother had struck him. It hissed and slithered and lunged at the stick with its fangs. After three more whacks, the snake's fight gave out and after three more, the snake was surely dead.

The two children eyed each other in triumph and lunged forward to eat their prize. The first bite held divine flavor. The juices burst from the peach skin to quench their thirst, and the fruit's soft meat melted in their mouths. They were impossible to eat neatly.

Soon, the children's faces and hands were covered in nectar. How many had each of them eaten? Five? Seven? Twelve?

Eve was silent. She seemed to have discovered a quiet contentment that Adam had rarely seen in his sister. Adam knew it was the fruit and wondered if they would ever taste anything so delicious again.

Without a word, the two children left the clearing, and Adam turned to take one last look at the tree. It remained full of fruit as if they hadn't plucked nearly a dozen peaches each. Something else was strange. While the fruit had regrown, the snake's carcass had vanished. Perhaps it had crawled away. Perhaps Eve had picked it up and thrown it in the woods without him noticing. Perhaps.

"Eve, did you..." Adam questioned his sister.

She interrupted him with a shrill scream. Her face turned pallid. Her pupils dilated. Adam turned around and saw what the snake had become. Up and up, his eyes absorbed the horror of the snake's transformed body. The red and black striped scales remained, but it stood taller than the surrounding bushes. Arms with hands—no, claws—had formed. Each claw quivered as the monster breathed heavily. Atop the broad shoulders, a face stared back at them. Its yellowing eyes narrowed and scanned. Fangs protruded from its mouth over human lips.

From the look of its mouth, the creature seemed to be smiling. But the smile did not reach the predator's eyes. It was devious, devilish, and filled with bloodlust.

"Run!" Adam yelled, grabbing his sister by the hand.

They knew how to run. They ran and they ran all the way back to their house, gasping as they slammed the door shut behind them.

Adam realized that the monster had never slithered an inch to chase them. Perhaps it didn't have to.

* * *

The bathwater was warm, made hot from a pail of well water brought to a boil over the fire. Mother bathed Adam and Eve together, like she did most nights. That night was no different, but really, it was.

"You two are quiet," Mother said as she scrubbed some dirt from behind Adam's ear with a bar of soap made from pig's fat.

"Nothing happened. We just played in the woods," Adam said. He hadn't yet perfected the art of lying, so the lie was much easier to see through than the sudsy bathwater.

"Oh?" Mother smiled. The Monster had taught Adam that a smile is not always friendly. "Nothing happened?" Mother asked.

Eve shook her head fervently. To Adam, it looked like too many shakes. Three or four might have been convincing. Twelve was too many.

"Eve?" Mother began, moving to her daughter with the bar of soap. Adam watched as Mother pinched his sister's arm. "Oww!" she cried.

"Oh, I'm sorry. I didn't mean to."

Adam turned his head and studied Mother inquisitively. He almost believed her, then considered her years of practice with lying.

"We...we..." Eve began to cry.

"Eve, no!" Adam said, kicking his sister's foot swiftly under the water.

Mother slapped Adam across the face. As tears welled in his eyes, so did anger in his heart, and the lump in his throat.

When Mother turned back to Eve, the crying girl told her the whole story. Panting and crying and panting and crying. Between what breaths she could take, she told the tale, leaving no stone unturned.

Mother listened stoically. Adam could scarcely hear her breathing, nor had he caught a blink in her eyes.

Eve concluded the story with a somber, "I'm sorry, Momma."

Mother stood and turned away from her two children. "You mustn't disquiet the fauna," she whispered. "It's our one rule. Our one rule you must follow."

"But it isn't," Adam said. "There are so many rules!"

Mother did not face her children. Her body was as stiff as a tree.

Her first son, Adam, continued, "We mustn't use electricity. We mustn't go into town. We mustn't read books other than scripture–"

"–You *mustn't* disquiet the fauna!" Mother screamed as she turned. Tears streamed down her face, reddening the whites of her eyes.

She lunged toward her two children in the bathtub and grabbed each of them by their head of hair. Adam clawed at his mother's arm, trying to escape with whatever fight he had. It was not enough.

She plunged her children's heads under the water and held them there.

Adam howled a muffled scream into the bathwater. As the air vacated his lungs, he thought of running. He ran far, far away from Eden. He ran through the valley, the forest, and over the mountains. He ran through Gatlinburg, then to Pigeon Forge. He ran to the very center of America and he screamed for the freedom that had been stolen from him. He ran as far as his little legs could carry. And then, when his lungs tired, he stopped.

The War-Forge
by David Ehrenman

The sword awakes in heat—   the homely fire
Couches the steel's   serene collapse.
With cleverness   the craftsman worn
Cares for the magma   molting as he
Masterfully creates   the cocoon.
Floating just below   the flaring surface
Bloody roses   ripple still
In folding layers   of liquefaction.
Tough the boy,   though yet untested,
Who grasps the hilt   and gazes on the blade.
Mesmerized by   prospects of memorial,
The boy permits himself   to hum softly
And place his name   in stead of heroes,
Songs of daring   and desperate times.
Good God forbid,   declares the gallant youth,
But if, perchance,   a peril comes to me,
I'll cry the battle-wail   and carry this to war.

The Moon Makes a Mockery

by Kevan Kenneth Bowkett

Once the Moon laughed at a boy—or so he thought. (It was really just wind-ripples in a moonlit pond.)

The boy plotted revenge against the Moon.

He tried to build things to reach the Moon with: a tower, a giant crossbow.

He failed.

The tower tumbled long before it reached the middle airs.

The crossbow's cord he was unable to draw back far enough to get any push, so taut was it. Once he did wind it back, and it slipped with his arm in the way—and his arm was dislocated. He had to abandon it after that.

When his arm healed he took to climbing the high mountains of the ice-girt southern ranges to try to reach the Moon, thinking that if the mocking planet lit anywhere on Earth it would be among those lofty frozen peaks. He scaled four of them; but each time he reached one of their summits the Moon was still as far away above him as when he stood on the low pampas.

"The Mocker comes here," he thought. "But it wishes to avoid me." And he shook his fist at the sky.

He took to wearing a wide-brimmed hat so he could not see the Moon, and stayed indoors on the three nights of the full. Because he felt a thirst for revenge possess him on those nights, and yet he had no way to act on it.

He went to the cities and to old temples and ancient inns, and poured over old manuscripts in moldering libraries, seeking the Moon's weaknesses.

He found three weaknesses mentioned in various texts of the arts magical.

The first mention was: *If you see the Moon's reflection in a pool of silver dragon's blood, this will give you power over it.*

But no one knew where a silver dragon was to be had, although he spent some time following the useless directions of idlers and wiseacres who knew less than he. Such creatures had reputedly been known in the old days, when the Empire was strewn with ice melting from the glaciation—but none had been seen for many hundreds of years.

The second mention of the Moon's weaknesses was: *If the Moon eclipses the Moon, you may bend it to your desire.*

But this seemed to him to refer to the time, long past, where to the world's familiar white moon Osi had been added Yeni, the Blue Moon, and Yisi, the Green. Only in those days could one of the satellites have eclipsed another. But those days were long gone.

"Yet are there not the Halls of Time in the palace of the Gods, which floats in the high airs?" he mused. "I might journey back to those lost ages and find such an eclipse as the texts speak of."

He sought Cymbar, the palace of the Gods: but as soon as he set his face in that direction he began to have bad luck, and this continued until things became ruinous—and only when he abandoned the plan did he notice his luck turn.

The third mention of how to harm the Moon was this: *Go and ask after the White Moon's undoing in the Wells of the Alliriyan, where sometimes wishes are granted and questions given answers.*

He journeyed to the Wells of the Alliriyan, far to the north in the continent of Senquaith, and descended into a well, deep down, though still he could perceive no bottom below him. And he asked a mist that floated in the well his question, how he might harm the Moon.

The mist coughed, and gave him an answer.

So he travelled further, to the tropical marshes beside the Sea of Gemuphanwa, and to a certain pool beneath three coconut palms that had grown twisted together.

There he waited—and he waited long, for he must see the Moon in the pool, and with the forest canopy and the heavy rains he seldom saw the sky.

Finally, on the 671st night of his vigil, he saw the faint smudge of the Moon in the water of the pool.

It floated there, seeming to mock him with its very indifference.

He had been told that whatever he did to the Moon's reflection in that pool would happen to the actual Moon.

He had been careful to bring many stones from the seashore. He threw the stones at the reflection of the Moon with all his might.

The glowing white Moon shattered and screamed.

He kept casting the stones. The Moon continued screaming and splintering as long as he had stones to hurl.

He exulted, he roared with each stone he drove into the shattered face of the Moon—at last his vengeance for the Moon's vicious mockery had come.

Finally he ran out of stones.

His arm was tired.

He looked at the pool—and as the broken water calmed he saw the Moon go back together again. In a moment it floated below him—and above him—as serenely as ever.

He cried out as if stabbed.

He wanted to hurt the Moon not for an hour, but for always.

He thought what he could do.

He thought long and he thought hard and he raked up all the great lore he had accumulated in his reading to bring to bear upon the problem.

And he realized what he had to do.

He made a Sun: and that put Moon in its place.

But then the Sun stuck its tongue out at him (or so he thought)....

Rolling Gurung Tampomas:
A Tale of West Java, Indonesia
by Annie McCann

'Ayo Annisa, it's your roll.' calls out Aditya.

Annisa rushes in, soda and chips in hand. Melati finishes her chocolate chip cookie as she takes notes for the next move. Annisa picks up the D20 dice, shaking it in her hand, hoping to beat Ahmad's last roll.

'HIT!' Aditya yells in his Dungeon master's voice.

'Well done, Annisa! One Komodo down, one to go,' Melati says.

The cold, wintry season of Western Sydney seeps through the windows, and sends a chill through the living room. The fireplace is all that is keeping Aditya and his friends warm during his new *Dungeons and Dragons* adventure. Unlike past quests, today is a quest through make-believe jungles of West Java, Indonesia to Gunung Tampomas, the rural town of Sumedang where players are to prevent a prophesised eruption from obliterating the town.

Aditya continues narrating. 'The second Komodo advances, claw by claw, a snarl escaping its lips, fierce fangs protruding its gums. It's hungry…'

Melati quivers in her seat.

'Ahmad, your roll,' Aditya calls. 'Will you use your bow and arrow to strike?'

Ahmad takes the dice, needing a 12 or higher. Fifteen… 'HIT!' The team cheers. 'With your D8 roll for damage, you've immobilised but not killed the Komodo.'

'We better run before the Komodo wakes,' Annisa says. She takes the D20.

'You now enter a saung,' Aditya continues. 'The bamboo shelter, providing shade. Your quest is far from over. Do we take a break or continue?'

Melati, Ahmad and Annisa look at each other.

'Let's take a break for real, back in 10,' says Melati rushing to the bathroom.

As the group disperses, Annisa explores the display of books and mesmerising carvings and sculptures of Indonesian mythology decorating the home library.

'Who else plays dice games?' Annisa asks Aditya.

'Just me,' he replies.

Annisa slowly pulls a dusty brown pouch from the shelf and hands it to Aditya. Melati and Ahmad walk in as a radiant glow lights up from inside the pouch.

Unlike dice Aditya collects, there is something special about these. Sparkles emit a vibe, deeper than a dice's ability to change the course of a game. He's never seen these before. Aditya pours the contents out of the pouch onto the nearby table. Everyone is awestruck with the range of intricately designed dice glistening before them.

Aditya has been teased often for his love of role-playing games. He is sure this pouch does not belong to his family.

Ahmad picks up a curiously colored marbled piece made of glass. Ice-cold to the touch, the exquisite shape could pass for dice. Colors begin to contrast upon each turn in his hand from red to white to red to white. 'A D10?' Ahmad examines it.

'I don't think that's dice,' Annisa says. She snatches it for closer examination. A shiver runs through her as she too experiences the ice-cold touch. 'Looks more like a diamond,' she says. She passes it to Melati who almost throws the freezing piece to Aditya.

A chill penetrates Aditya's skin, and it feels remarkably like pins and needles stabbing his hand through to his fingers. Aditya bites his tongue and holds the dice firmly while studying it, noticing for the first time there are no engravings. No numbers or even carved-in dots like other gaming dice. Colors start contrasting again from red to white then to black. The dice suddenly changes from ice cold to heat, scorching his hand. Aditya drops it on the table, watching it bounce around before centering itself in the middle.

Silence ensues as everyone looks at Aditya.

'I don't know what happened,' he whispers. 'It almost burnt a hole in my palm.'

Everyone watches the dice expectantly when the table starts vibrating, sending waves through to the carpet, shaking everyone to the floor.

'What is happening?' Melati screams.

Swirling colours of smoke emerge from the dice, transforming from pink to smoky red and white, thickening by the second, encapsulating the room.

Everyone struggles to remain on their feet. The earth rumbles again, shaking everyone intensely. Books Annisa was marveling over only moments ago fall to the floor. The chandelier above sways from left to right, threatening to crash down upon everyone at any moment.

Aditya, the first to regain balance, notices a change in their surroundings. The dining table, once supporting their role-playing game board, now becomes a marble stone tabletop. The kitchen, once a storage haven for tea pots and crockery, now is a dense, tropical jungle. Upon each turn of his head, the once cozy living room grows lush foliage of green dense jungle. A stifling humidity penetrates the air, seeping through his clothes and skin.

An eerie silence takes over when the group notice a ten-foot-long scaly-skinned, bow-legged creature encroaching their space. Its flat head looking down upon them like prey with its yellow two-pronged tongue sticking out of its mouth, threating to spit venom at any moment.

This is not a hallucination.

Its muscular, long tail swishes behind it, strong enough to knock anyone out.

'Komodo…' Annisa says in a low tone.

They're face to face with one of Indonesia's largest predators. Ordinarily thriving in harsh, tropical climates of the Sunda Islands, the Komodo dragon inches closer, claws scratching the ground.

'Do not move or make a sound,' Annisa whispers.

'Have you lost your mind? Run!' Melati says shakily.

'No, she's right. If we run, it will give chase,' Ahmad says.

The monstrous creature steps closer, its violating horrid breath inches away from them. An ear-piercing wail shatters the silence as Melati sees a python slithering down a nearby tree trunk. Without another thought, they break into a run, trudging through thick, swampy jungle, the damp ground making it a challenge to run any faster.

Ahmad trips over a jungle vine, slamming headfirst into the ground. Annisa stops, turns back, and helps Ahmad off the ground when the Komodo dragon suddenly pauses. Annisa locks eyes with the Komodo dragon, a secret understanding passing through them – she killed its companion. She tries to anticipate its next move when the creature rushes at them, two grey-scaled feet at a time.

'Ayo! Bendiri!' Annisa commands Ahmad to stand.

The Komodo dragon closes in, its elongated, muscular tail swishes behind as it springs forward, narrowly missing Annisa and Ahmad. The Komodo dragon lands on all fours, releasing a frightening growl rumbling the ground throughout the jungle. The monster looks back at Annisa, drool dripping from its snout, then runs off in the opposite direction, leaving nothing but pawprints on the muddy ground.

Ahmad and Annisa help each other up, checking for cuts and bruises.

'Where's Aditya?' Annisa pants.

'Right here,' Aditya croaks, sneaking from behind Melati.

'Someone care to explain what is going on?' Ahmad tries to catch his breath.

The location appears obvious as everyone takes in the green foliage and soaks in the humidity while swatting mosquitos away. But it raises more questions than answers.

Aditya tries to collect himself as memories return piece by piece.

'There is something weird about that pouch,' Annisa says, recalling the glistening dice she pulled from the shelf.

Aditya and Ahmad nod—remembering the icy mystery with contrasting colours.

'It was like holding a vibrating ice cube that started stabbing my hand,' Aditya recalls.

Drops of rain sprinkle from the sky, a welcome respite for the heat. Raindrops soon turns into torrential rain. With no map, no direction or even a phone to call home, everyone continues trudging aimlessly through endless jungle.

'Over here!' Ahmad points toward a cave in the cliffside where everyone follows.

The smell of fresh rain wafts through the cave, a calming breeze in its wake as the downpour drenches the jungle.

'You know what I think?' Ahmad offers. 'You rolled a dice and the quest you wrote up for us came to life.'

Aditya shrugs, something tells him Ahmad is right.

Another gentle breeze floats through the cave, gently putting everyone to sleep.

A squawk shrieks through the air, waking everyone from their slumber in the cave. A large eagle sits on the mountain top, looking upon the valley. A creature so majestic, its golden aura radiates off its feathers. Opening its magnificent wings it soars to the sky, momentarily blocking the sun, creating an eerie darkness. They group watch the celestial bird, as it perches on the ground. A golden aura surrounds its divinity, lighting up the dark, dense jungle.

Standing at full height, golden scales covering its legs, the eagle boasts the torso and arms of a strong man with golden skin. Its red wings with long, glimmering feathers spread from its back, stretching a mile wide.

Mesmerized, Aditya steps forward, eyeing the human face with the beak of a divine eagle. A golden crown sits upon the creature's head, snake necklaces adorning its neck like trophies. He has seen this creature before he just can't remember where.

'MAKE IT STOP!' Melati cries, blocking her ears.

Aditya hears it too. A deep, commanding voice infiltrating his mind.

I mean you no harm, it says.

Everyone blocks their ears except for Aditya who faces the magnificent beast as it continues communicating telepathically.

I am Garuda. Half-brother of Devas, Gandharvas, Daityas, Danavas, Nagas, Vanara and Yakshas. Son of the sage Kashyapa and Vinata. Younger brother of Aruna the charioteer of the Sun.

Garuda, the king of birds Aditya remembers. The protector not aggressor with power to travel fast and destroy its enemy—the serpent, which explains the snake necklaces.

I can take you from here if you will trust me.

Aditya bows his head to Garuda, offering his respect and acceptance.

Climb aboard me, I will transport you, Garuda voices through their minds. *I will guide and protect you from here.* Garuda bows, waiting for everyone to climb on but no one moves.

'You know, I read somewhere, Garuda was known to be the Hindu god Vishnu's trusted mode of transportation,' Aditya says.

'Works for me.' Melati proceeds toward Garuda.

'Try not to pull too hard on the feathers,' Annisa says as she climbs aboard.

Garuda rockets into the air, surpassing the mountain top.

'Great job Aditya, first rolling the dice that got us here now accepting rides from a stranger creature having no idea where it'll take us,' Ahmad grunts.

'You could have stayed in the cave,' Aditya retorts.

'Cool it, you two. Besides, I found that dice, not Aditya,' Annisa says.

Dropping in altitude, the smell of the tropics awash once again, as they come in for landing in the middle of a Sawah. Garuda gradually slows, landing smoothly in the rice paddy field, splashing all aboard. The open landscape green and swampy.

Wilujeng sumping di Gunung Tampomas, Sumedang, says Garuda, welcoming everyone in Sundanese dialect.

The glorious Tampomas mountain stands before them, elevated thousands of meters above sea level, surrounded by lush green.

'I have been here before,' Aditya says. 'My Dad was born in Sumedang, we came here to visit family. Gunung Tampomas is a volcano, it gets a lot of tourists. Why are we here?'

Garuda leads them to the saung, bamboo shelter providing shade from tropical heat then expresses itself through open divine wings. Its golden feathers reflect brightly off the rays of the sun.

'Oh no, here it goes again,' Melati covers her ears.

'You know it is speaking through our minds, not our ears,' Aditya says.

Sumedang was known as the Kingdom of Sumedang Larang, the land of fertile soil, abundance of flowing water and prosperous nature. People never hungered and everyone was happy. The mountain, you see, Garuda points its beak to the mountainous terrain across the sawah, *was once known as Gunung Gede, Large Mountain. Before you can continue the journey, you need to know the story of Gunung Gede.*

'Journey? What journey!?' says Ahmad in exasperation.

A sudden roar from the mountain shook the land, Garuda continues. *The people fled. News of this unusual activity made its way to the wise young king who was scared for the safety of his people. He meditated for guidance and a magical whisper ordered him to throw a golden keris belonging to his ancestors into the crater of Gunung Gede.*

By feeding the mountain with the golden dagger, it should appease it and all will be safe. As the legend goes, the young king, indeed threw the golden keris into the crater and the mountain was renamed Gunung Tampomas— the mountain receiving gold.

However, unusual rumbles started again, threatening to destroy Sumedang. It is said the golden keris, once thrown into the crater was a replica. Gunung Tampomas was fooled and is angry. I searched high and low for truth. I know now, the only one who can stop this is the descendant of the King of Sumedang.

Ahmad bursts into laughter. 'Descendant of royalty? Sorry to disappoint you, grand bird, but none of us here can help so if this mountain is going to blow, we are in its direct path. Thank you so much for bringing us—'

One of you rolled the sacred stone, Garuda ignores Ahmad. *The stone of eminence, life and purity. The stone with colours of sacrifice and struggle. Only a descendant from the King of Sumedang Larang has the power to roll the sacred stone and open the portal.*

Everyone looks to a shocked Aditya.

'I didn't roll it, I dropped accidentally,' he says.

You must bring the golden keris of your ancestors to Gunung Tampomas and throw it into the crater, Garuda concludes.

46

Aditya keels over, unable to breathe. The discovery of his ancestral truth and new responsibility unbearable. Garuda is not helping them, he was seeking help and Aditya is the chosen one.

I searched for centuries and finally located the golden keris. I kept it hidden from enemies. Garuda pulls out the golden keris from under its wing and hands it to Aditya. *I knew one of you would be the descendant of the King of Sumedang when I saw the earth change as you stepped towards the cave.*

Garuda hands Aditya the golden keris who accepts it with shaky hands, admiring the exquisite craftmanship of intricately carved patterns swirling along the golden sheath. The hilt resembling the beak of Garuda with a distinct double-edged curvy blade.

Only you can throw this. Garuda looks at Aditya. *We do not have a lot of time before Gunung Tampomas unleashes the full extent of its wrath.*

Aditya's face drains of color. Melati and Annisa comfort him, offering words of support and strength. A skeptical Ahmad still blames Aditya for their predicament.

'How do we know Aditya is powerful enough to wield that dagger?'

Garuda steps towards Ahmad, so intimidating as its claws digging into the ground.

I don't doubt your fears, but you will do well to remember I am not wrong.

Ahmad gulps, retreating towards his friends.

'Maafkan saya,' Aditya apologises, realising he must make this trip alone. 'Please forgive me. I had no idea. My family never told me.'

Melati and Annisa pull Aditya into a hug, unable to hold back tears. A hesitant Ahmad joins, clapping Aditya on his back before he follows in the footsteps of his ancestor and climbs aboard Garuda.

I can only take you to the edge, from there you must proceed alone, Garuda says as they sore into the sky towards the smoking Gunung Tampomas.

Tremors continue as Aditya struggles to stand. Lava bubbles below as white smoke billows from within. The stench of sulphur making it difficult for Aditya to focus as he attempts to throw the golden keris. Another violent tremor knocks him over, the golden keris falling out of his hand, clambering onto stone edges.

The tremors and smell of sulphur intensify as Aditya tries to adjust his vision. A golden gleam catches his eye. The golden keris balancing on the edge of the stone, almost tipping over. Aditya crawls across ledge when the mountain shakes once more and the golden keris slips. With a last bout of strength, Aditya lunges forward catching it before it falls to the valley.

An emotional Aditya rolls on his back trying to catch his breath, closing his eyes for a moment when a man enters in a vision wearing brown and black batik sarung, emerald-green vest and golden crown atop a traditional West Javanese bendo wrapped around his head. The man's face is blurred but a deep voice speaks to Aditya telepathically.

Hatur Nuhun, thank you.

Aditya's eyes spring open. He is alone on the mountain. *Who was that?* As the mountain roars, Aditya reaches his arm as far back as he can and throws the golden keris into the crater. The golden keris lands in the lava with a splash. A soft growl and puff of smoke comes from the mountain before rumblings ease and silence follows. Nothing but chirping birds echo across the jungle. Smoke recedes into volcano like clouds moving in reverse. Aditya takes in slow, deep breaths as his eyes droop before losing all consciousness.

Hatur Nuhun, the deep voice returns.

As though he is in a dream but awake at the same time, Aditya is draped in a white towel like material, standing in the middle of white, barren land facing Garuda and a regal man.

Your great sacrifice saved Sumedang. The mountain received the true golden keris and Gunung Tampomas has accepted. The King and I both thank you. Hatur Nuhun.

Aditya's eyes flutter open. The oxygen mask so tight, he tries to pull it off. A disoriented Aditya takes in his surroundings, his friends by his side.

'Ssh, you're okay,' Melati soothes. 'You're in hospital.'

Annisa nods. 'Just before you left, Garuda cast our minds to sleep. We all woke in your living room, you didn't so we brought you here.'

Aditya doesn't know what to say other than smile, grateful to be back with his friends.

'So, same time next week at yours, Aditya?' Ahmad chuckles.

Aditya sighs. 'No… I think I am done with quests for a while.'

Disenchantment

by Jacob Bier

Do you recall, when we were young,
The distant songs of fairy land?
But now they are not often sung,
Something I still don't understand.

Did those old songs exhaust their power?
Did all their magic fade away?
Do they, after their golden hour,
Have nothing left to teach or say?

Perhaps instead we've lost the ear
To hear such music anymore;
Grown old and dull, we do not care
To sit in silence, waiting for

The sound of pan pipes on the breeze,
The din of elfin drums and flutes;
We've left the wisdom of the trees
And lost the innocence of youth.

For all our years, we're far worse off
Than we admit, more than we fear;
Senseless and dumb, we're blind and deaf
To signs and wonders everywhere.

But every now and then I hear
A distant tune or melody
That calls me back to yesteryear
And wakes again the child in me.

The Minotaur

by Robert Thomas

The maiden quivered on the cold, hard stone, huddled in a dark corner of a dark passage. She pulled her knees close and gathered in the ragged wool stola that was her only comfort. She was sure the passage came to an end here. If it found her she could not flee. But maybe it knew this was a dead end, and it would not come here. Who would hide here, helpless, with no place to run? Her legs might not carry her anyway. She had mostly crawled through the stinking, filthy, sightless hallways. It seemed safer.

Her stomach pinched. Her mouth was dry and chalky. Maybe she could die of hunger and thirst before it found her.

She sat, against the stone, curled tight, shaking. Sometimes, exhausted sleep would overtake her for a few moments before she was pulled back into the dark terror. Her eyes had gradually adjusted. She could just make out the mottled walls of the passages, discern corners and turns. Sometimes, she could recognize, and smell, a mound, a corpse, cut down she knew not when, but in some stage of rot, and she beat away the flies. This is when she would climb to her feet and walk upright a short distance, to escape the stench and the bugs, her arms outstretched, before collapsing back down on her bloody knees, and crawling on.

And now she huddled in the cold finality of a dead end, in a corner of Daedalus' cruel, rough-hewn stone.

She was fading into another tormented sleep.

She heard a sudden huff.

A long, powerful nasal exhalation that shattered the dark, still, noisome air. Then a long, sucking inhale. Almost thoughtful.

The maiden's whole body became stone. Her jaw dropped and she could feel her eyes widen, involuntarily. She slowed down her breathing. If only she could pull in her stink and sweat and hide it. Her stola was white, like a maiden's. She hoped the crawling and slinking and sleeping on filthy stone had turned it black, like the air.

She just stared at the opposite wall of the passage. She heard several light steps. Her chest pounded. Please, Athena, she pleaded silently, let this be quick. Give me a quick end. Another bellowing exhalation, louder now, hard and determined. Sweat oozed over the maiden's white skin. She trembled. She could hear it breathing, smell its filthy stench. She turned her head, slowly. She should not have chosen to hide here. Her eyes gaped into the dark.

She could see the faint outline.

A large man. Broad. Tall. Naked. Muscular. Covered in hair. From its wide shoulders, a man transformed. For human flesh gave way to the folding muscles of a massive, furry bovine neck, and this continued to the large, bloated, menacing head, and black eyes and flaring nostrils and jutting horns, of a mighty bull. The *tauros*.

The maiden's throat hardened. She choked back her breath in sputters, her mouth parched and gaping. She pulled tightly against her knees. It stepped forward again, and looked down upon her crumpled, quivering form. In its right hand it held a broad, flat stone.

The maiden remembered what her mother had said to her before she and the six other maidens and seven youths, all of the best family, all chosen by lot, boarded the sacrificial boat in satisfaction of the grim yearly tribute to King Minos of Crete. Do not scream, she said, as they hugged and cried. You are a maiden of Athens. Do not scream. Pray to our goddess for a quick end and a long eternity by her side at the feasting table of Olympus. Do not scream.

It stood. Menacing. She huddled. Helpless. It suddenly opened its maw and a huge, slimy tongue slapped around before being sucked back, sending forth a stench that smelled like putrid flesh.

The maiden could not scream. Her mouth moved up and down as she tried to force a breath out of tightened innards. She must not scream. She is a maiden of Athens.

"I'm Daphne," she forced out in a choked whisper. She licked her lips. Then slightly louder, "I'm Daphne."

She knew not what else to say. She could not scream.

She looked at its hand holding the wide, flat rounded stone. It didn't move. The beast stood there, looking down at her with large, dark eyes.

Then she remembered. The story of the bull was well-known. The impiety of King Minos. His cursed wife.

"Asterion?" the maiden said, softly. "Asterion? Is that your name? I'm Daphne."

It looked down at her and twisted its massive neck slightly. Then it let out another deep breath from flaring nostrils.

The maiden swallowed hard, painfully. She loosened. Let her arms fall from her knees, gently, to the cold stone blocks. She pushed her legs out, slightly.

"Asterion? Will you sit with me?"

Its ears twitched. It looked away. Another, softer nasal grunt. It looked back at her. And the maiden stared into its big, deep eyes. She gently stretched out a shaking hand, not to the beast, but to the hard floor beside her.

A long moment passed.

The beast dropped the stone.

It turned its back to the wall. It slowly lowered its hulking form down along the rough surface, and sat, leaning against the stone, looking at the wall opposite, as the maiden had done for so long.

The maiden let out a long, low silent breath, and then inhaled slowly. She needed to be calm. She tried to stop shaking. She had not screamed. She was alive.

It just sat against the wall, beside her. Another long moment. The sweat against the maiden's skin started to dry and she was getting cold.

She licked her lips again, trying to find saliva in her aching throat, and swallowed. "Asterion, your father shut you up in this place. Made you do-"

No, she must not make him feel guilty. Wicked. Irredeemable.

"Your father put you here. You cannot help who you are, Asterion. But he put you here.

Down here in the dark. To live in this horrible place. In these tangled passages." It let out another big nasal breath.

It sounded like a sigh.

She looked sideways at its great head. It was matted and caked and reeking. Probably coated with blood. She thought, it had to ram its victims with its head and horns. And how could it tear human flesh with the flat teeth of a bull? Wretched.

And she could see into the one eye. Deep and empty. Was it looking at her?

She adjusted herself and her stola, slightly, toward the beast. It noticed. It turned its head and shoulders, slightly, toward her. It's hands were on the cold floor too.

She gulped and took a deep breath.

"Asterion. We should go back to Athens. We should try to find our way out of here. And find some of the others who--"

She stopped again. How many had it already devoured? She took another deep breath.

"If we can find our way out of this place, we can sail back to Athens. You can save me. And anyone else we find along the way. You can live in Athens. They will not hold you at fault. And you can eat grass, oats, wild flowers, Asterion. And drink pure water. And live in the sun and the fields."

She was breathing hard. She thought of something else. She smiled in the dark.

"And Asterion. If it is your will, your pleasure, you can sail back here with the Athenian host and unseat your wicked father who put you here. You would look fine in shiny bronze armor, Asterion. Bearing a spear, not a stone. And you can eat the grass and oats of Crete. In freedom."

The beast looked down to the cold floor for a while. It then inclined its head slightly more towards the maiden. And from its nostrils came a long, low breath. And from its throat came a low, guttural grunt.

The maiden swallowed. The sweat started to flow from her skin again. She slowly raised the hand that was closest to the beast. Slowly, so it could see it with its big eye. And placed the white, stained, stone-sanded hand on the creature's massive cheek. And just rested it there. She felt the dirt and the matted grime. It did not move. But its eye blinked and twitched.

And they sat there. Its nasal breath long and slow.

She had not screamed. She was alive.

The glimmer of light came suddenly, from around a sharp corner out of the endless twisting passage. The beast fumbled for his flat stone and jerked himself up clumsily. The light expanded to a glowing cloud. A man turned the corner and stopped as if languidly searching for something, holding a torch out before him. He saw them and stepped forward. The maiden pushed herself up off the floor with weak legs, one hand against the stone wall. She felt a sharp, searing rush of excitement. They both squinted against the torchlight.

The man stood tall and straight and furious. He wore a knee-length, purple cloak, clasped at the waist by a leather belt with a golden buckle. A scabbard hung by his side. Curly blond hair with a golden band framed a handsome, dark, determined face. His feet were clad with fine leather sandals. In one hand, the torch. In the other, a large spool of thick red yarn on a spindle. The yarn trailed behind him.

The maiden looked hard past the torchlight.

"My prince!" she shrieked. "Prince Theseus! Prince of Athens! You have come!" He did not look at her. He looked at the beast.

"I have come, young maiden," he replied sharply. Then gritting his teeth, "I have come."

He dropped the spool of yarn and quickly drew his sword. The wide polished bronze glimmered. He gripped the torch tightly at his side. He put one leg forward in battle stance as the beast, suddenly cornered, lowered his massive head and made ready to charge, emitting a long, mean guttural bellow. The maiden looked at the beast and at the hero. And then at the beast. She rushed forward and put herself between the two, facing Theseus, her arms outstretched beside her.

"My prince, do not slay the beast!"

"Stand aside, young maiden! Do not get in its way! It will trample you!"

"It will not trample me, my prince. It saved me. It spared me."

"Stand aside!"

"My prince," she moaned, now extending her arms forward to Theseus in supplication, "I implore you. The beast is not evil. It is a pathetic victim. Born of unnatural deeds. Shut in here by a cruel father who exacted the abominable tribute from our city. It did not. It has wandered, starving and cold in this place just like its victims. It does not wish to kill again. He does not wish to kill again!"

Theseus' glared at the maiden and pointed his sword towards her.

"Young maiden, I too have wandered this dark, sickening labyrinth and found half-eaten corpses. Hacked and mangled by that stone he wields. Our youths. Our maidens. You would have been one of those. After the third sacrifice, the third ship, which you boarded with the rest, wailing, I implored the king my father, King Aegeus of Athens, to send me here, to put an end to this gruesome tribute and our subjugation. Stand aside, dear maiden. You are weak and hysterical."

The maiden buried her head in her hands and cried loudly.

"No, my prince. He did not wish this. Do not hold him at fault. I told him he was not condemned to this. I called him by name. He did not kill me. He sat with me."

"He sat with you?"

She cried and sniffled into her hands, then looked up at the prince.

"I told him he could eat oats and grass and wild flowers in Attica. I told him he could put on amour and join the host that would unseat his wicked father. Please, my prince!"

She sobbed and coughed, hunched over. Theseus furled his brow and smiled wryly.

The beast tossed away his flat stone and went down on one knee and bowed his head low and placed his outstretched hands on the stone floor and let out a low, gentle grunt. The maiden turned to him, then turned back to Theseus, smiling through filthy tears.

"Do you see, my prince? You cannot slay a supplicant. He is contrite. He is a victim. No less than we were. He saved me. You saved us. Let there be no more bloodshed. It is impious, my lord, to slay a supplicant. Do not slay him!"

She stretched out her arms again to the prince. They stood. Theseus looked back and forth from the maiden to the pathetic, almost prostrate beast before him. He thought. He sighed. He lowered his sword. Stillness. He sheathed it with a frustrated thud.

"Very well, young maiden. You are right that it is impious to kill a supplicant. I cannot bring the wrath of the gods upon my house."

He paused, looking down at the beast.

"And you are right that he was shut up cruelly in this place, fed youths and maidens by the tyrant king of Crete, not because the beast desired it, but to preserve his own power, setting Athens as an example to any who might oppose him."

The maiden sighed heavily and then herself went down on one knee.

"Oh my prince, you are just," she sniffled. "And you will be a just king. This act of justice will lift you up over all other kings."

"Rise, maiden. And you too, bull of Minos. Rise before your prince and lord and future king. And mark, while the maiden has won me over and I spare you, the merest violence from you and I will cut you down without a thought."

The beast raised his massive head and slowly lifted himself upright. He looked at the prince, and grunted gently. In the torchlight now, the maiden and the hero cold see his full grotesque and repulsive form. His body, though muscular, was yet rather emaciated, tired and scratched and weary, covered in filthy matted hair, his hands worn and twisted and his nails black. His neck and head were caked with dirt and blood and gore that stuck to his long, sharp horns and jagged ears. The beast noticed them staring, and lowered his head again.

"He smells, maiden."

"Yes, my prince."

"Young maiden, we must try to find the others. Those he has not devoured. And then we must leave. My father is on watch for me at Cape Sounion. We will change my sail from black to white, to signify my safe return."

As the prince spoke, the maiden noticed another light emerging even more quickly from the passage.

"My prince, behind. Another comes."

Theseus turned toward the passage, one eye on the beast, and placed his hand on his scabbard.

A young woman appeared, lightly panting. A noble woman, tall and shapely. She carried a torch and a spear. She was dressed in a bright white gown with purple edges, cinched with a purple sash. On her head, a tiara. On her arms, flashing bangles. Around her slender neck, gold chain. Her feet well shod. Her skin white and soft. She held up her torch.

"Ariadne," Theseus protested, "why did you come here? What are you doing?"

The maiden beheld the noblewoman transfixed. The beast stood still.

"I could not linger any longer at the entrance to this place, my lord. You had been gone a while. I might be seen. I followed you. I followed the trail of thick red yarn as fast as I could. To be with you."

She looked at the beast with a furrow.

"My lord?"

He swallowed.

"My lady, the beast is a supplicant. He is subdued. The maiden tamed him and he prostrated himself before me. It is impious to slay a supplicant. We shall take him. He is unnatural. That is not his fault. He was shut up in this place against his will by your cruel father. He too is a victim. We will take him to Athens."

The noblewoman stood frozen. Ariadne looked at Theseus.

"Maiden, you know Ariadne is daughter to the tyrant King Minos. We met here. We will be married. She too will leave this place and come to Athens. She will be my queen. Your queen. His queen. She gave me the spool of yarn, maiden, that I could find and kill the beast and then make my way back out of this twisted dungeon."

Ariadne stepped forward slowly and approached the beast. He stepped back a little. She approached further, resting her spear on the ground, gawking at him in the torchlight. A gentle smile curled her red-painted lips.

"Asterion," she said slowly and breathlessly.

The beast blinked and twitched his nostrils.

"My half-brother. You are wretched and filthy and bloody. Yes, you have suffered. I remember you as a boy, Asterion, unnatural and clumsy, your vast appetite, your fearsome strength, how you became more and more ungovernable."

"My princess," said the maiden, "now he will eat oats and grass and wild flowers in the fields of Attica."

Ariadne paid no heed to the maiden.

"You are black with grime, my half-brother. Your father the great bull was pure white. The finest bull ever. Sent to my father by Poseidon. For sacrifice. You had a beautiful white head and neck too. I used to stroke your head and neck, when you were young. Soft white fur."

A moment of silence fell.

Leaning on her spear, she turned her head to Theseus, her face suddenly red.

"Would that my selfish father the king had sacrificed the bull as Poseidon commanded!" She spat out the words in anger. "How can one fool the gods? And then my mother the witch Pasiphae struck with unnatural lust for the beautiful white beast, a curse from the sea god in retribution. How ignoble, my lord!" She clenched her face in fury. "And she got that sycophant Daedalus to build her a wooden heifer!" She looked back at the beast. "And all this. This outrage, these cruel sacrifices, this bloody, cursed island!"

Theseus took a step forward.

"And now it ends, my lady."

She smiled again at the beast. "My brother," she said plaintively, "Asterion."

She quickly slid her right hand down the smooth shaft of her spear and thrust it forward into the beast's heart, tossing away the torch. He fell back against the wall with a bursting, painful bovine shriek from the depths of his flaring nostrils.

"Now it ends, my lord!" she yelled, wide eyes bulging from her red grimacing face. "It is not my supplicant and it cannot live!" With both hands and her whole body she thrust forward, burying the shaft deeper.

Theseus lunged forward. "Ariadne!" He seized her from behind with his free arm, the other grasping his torch, to pull her away.

The maiden fell to her knees, "Noooo, princess!"

Ariadne continued with all her might to thrust the spear forward, lowering her head and haunching her shoulders.

"This abomination cannot live my lord!" she sputtered uncontrollably. "My brother and my shame! Our shame! We are to be married!"

The beast slid down the rough stone wall, trailing a stain of blood, and collapsed on the rock floor. He stretched his mighty head back in agony, grabbing at the shaft. Then he reached an arm for the maiden and bent his neck to her, while the enraged princess continued to thrust.

"Ariadne!" yelled the hero furiously, "let go the spear, Ariadne!" She let go suddenly and he threw her back on to the stone floor. He pulled the spear out of the beast. A pool of thick blood formed on the stones. He tossed the spear aside angrily.

The maiden wailed. "Oh princess of Crete, why?" She scurried over to the beast and knelt beside him and tried to cup his massive head in her hands. The beast looked at her, let out a final, desperate groan, and fell silent, those big dark eyes staring lifeless.

Theseus turned back to the princess and yelled, "a fine act of sympathy for your wretched brother, woman!"

"That was my cruel fate, my lord," she replied sharply, raising herself off the ground. "The abomination could not live." She brushed off her white gown and straightened her tiara and picked up her torch. "We are leaving Crete and will be married." She lifted her chin, proud and noble. "And you, my lord, will have the glory of slaying the beast and liberating the youth of Athens. And your city shall be free. And your rule assured."

The maiden wept, placing her head gently on the beast's oozing breast.

Theseus glared at his princess. She stood unmoved. Then his face softened. "Very well, my lady. You have done your deed. And as you say, I have done mine. I have slain the monster and freed Athens and we shall be married and rule. Now let us leave this hellish place." He picked up the spool of yarn. "Maiden, come."

"My lord?"

"Yes, Ariadne?"

"You must be undoubted slayer of the monster."

He turned to the princess. She nodded to the weeping maiden. "You must have the glory. The undoubted glory of slaying the monster. You came into the labyrinth with my spool of yarn and you slew the monster and saved the youths and maidens of Athens and became king."

Theseus twisted his faced in anguish. She looked back at him with a face of stone. Then he looked at the maiden, who had lifted her head from the beast and sat next to him, smeared all over with his blood, her face black with dirt and tears, looking at them, wide-eyed.

Theseus stepped forward to the maiden, and looked down at her. "Sweet maiden, what is your name?"

She looked up at her prince, trembling. "Daphne."

A moment passed.

"Daphne," said the prince, softly.

He drew his sword. The maiden screamed.

The Craftsman's Bane
by S. R. Horgan

A sliver of oak curled upon itself, broke from the old man's planer, and spiraled to the ground. The earthy smell of resin pleased him, and he inhaled deeply. He cleared the mouth of the planer and leaned forward again, letting all his weight rest in perfect balance on his hand, all the force of his still-strong muscles distill into the delicate edge of the blade. A few minutes later he stopped to rest. He blew on the panels to clear them of sawdust. There was still one blank place untouched by his planer, but apart from this one small thing, all the other scenes on the door panels for the shrine would soon be complete.

He heard the fisherman's quiet steps stop behind him in the sand. He set his tools down, wiped the shavings from his hands, and turned to get up. The old seaman extended his hand downward just as he had the day they met, the day Daedalus had been floundering in the sea, framed by hundreds of loose white feathers. Wordlessly, Daedalus took his hand and pulled himself up. As he followed the fisherman along the shoreline, he glanced to the west. The sun's blinding white reflection on dark water was like a path pointing back to Crete, a path that would move as the sun moved, always beyond reach.

The sun had set on that sea many times since the sea had set on Icarus, but Daedalus did not count days now when time was so far subjected to pain. Time was only the medium for grief. Each day he came to the beach, sneaking away from the old couple who had taken him in, unable to bear their kindness and the quiet life they lived for too long. But he was learning to.

The waves were calm that evening, just as they had been when the old seaman had pulled Daedalus half-drowned from the scene of blood and broken wings that floated like flotsam. In the moment of rescue, the slowness of Daedalus's speech, which he had always felt as a burden on his own tongue and his listeners' ears too, rendered him unable to make the confession waterlogging his heart. He could not fight the old man's hands lifting under his armpits any more than he could swim, and so he was saved. It was too late for Icarus. Neither the fisherman nor his wife had ever asked Daedalus what happened.

Inside the cottage, the fisherman's wife pushed bowls of soup towards the two men without a word. Her fingers were as gnarled as her husband's white eyebrows, but when Daedalus lifted the bowl to his lips, he saw the deep wrinkles mapping his own hands. The soup was delicious. The old woman watched him as he lifted it to his mouth to drink the last drops.

After dinner he joined the fisherman on his boat, as he had every night since that first.

Tacking across Icarus's burial ground, Daedalus wondered how he could have been so blind. When the boy was born, Daedalus had looked upon him with resolve. He planned to teach his son everything he knew and offer him the chance to be great. As Icarus grew, Daedalus took on an attitude of detachment that he thought was noble and self-effacing and that would replace the piercing envy that had led him to do terrible, terrible things in the past. It worked too well. Through the dual suppression of his love along with his offenses, he only taught Icarus how to ignore the wounds of the heart; that was all he really knew. Daedalus was supposed to be the seer, but how little he saw his own pride, his own reckless ambition, his own sins.

It was hard to understand what had happened at first, that day that was supposed to be the day of liberation. The ascent; the stamped silhouette of Icarus's body against the sun; the rapid, whirling, chaotic fall. When Daedalus still thought his son might pull out of the tailspin, he rehearsed the way he would chastise him once they were safely back on land: *Who taught you to believe that you could outrun your own foolishness? Who made you believe that a man could bring even the sun to heel?* At first, Daedalus actually asked those questions seriously. Later, when all was said and done, he realized he knew the answer.

But a more honest question haunted him for a long time afterwards. It was simply, *Why didn't he listen to me when I warned him of the perils of flying too high?* Daedalus asked himself this question hundreds of times a day, and a thousand times a day he imagined how things would have ended if Icarus had listened to his directions before they left the tower. They would have begun a new life together, and he would have been a better father, finally, in some happy place far away from Crete. *Why didn't he listen to me?* But Daedalus finally realized that his son had stopped listening long before that fateful day, because his father had not said anything worth listening to. And even worse, Daedalus had stopped listening to him.

Before they had leapt from their tower prison that day, on the very wings of hope, Daedalus had dwelled there reticently. He had refused to believe that Icarus was strong enough to know the truth, to know *him*. Daedalus had not understood how keeping the secrets of his past had reinforced the walls that entrapped his son.

By the time Daedalus and the fisherman brought in the tuna and cleaned them, it was dark. Daedalus washed his hands and settled down in his little shack. Sometimes the long days helped him to sleep quickly, but that night the figures he had carved in the oak panels rose up before him, and the one untouched section haunted him. He had smoothed it with his callused palms dozens of times, as if his hands alone could bring the wood to life. But whenever grief for Icarus led him to that point, he stepped back with a deep breath and allowed himself the possibility that the gap on the panels might never be filled.

Once before, he thought he had brought wood to life. Across the sea in Crete, in murky light and a weedy field, tatty leather still hung off a skeletal frame. When the heat was oppressive and the sun's glare on the water was too bright in Daedalus's eyes, he closed them only to find stamped on his eyelids the image of that incubator of magic, that machine that would generate inky lawlessness and reveal the shabby clothes of all the gods before. Like a mirage, he saw that most awful altar that he had fashioned for Pasiphaë's lust. And it looked like a gallows on the grassy plane.

The fisherman seemed to know when his companion was caught up in memories from another, painful world. He would bump Daedalus's shoulder and hand him the flask of freshwater, and Daedalus would blink away all remembrance of his part in bringing the Minotaur demigod to life, all the greed and pride that had driven him, and all the pain and suffering his creation had caused. Instead, he would fix his gaze on the beautiful blue sea. And they would lower their nets one more time, and one more time again, until the sun was long bedded.

Now, staring up at the ceiling of reeds, Daedalus wished that he could close his eyes and dream without nightmares. Not yet—but someday—how he wished that he could believe in mercy.

It was not a night for sleeping, so Daedalus left the shack and crept out towards the quietly lapping waves.

With tenderness he remembered the young boy who loved to play in the soil, building fortresses in clay and sand. He pictured the precocious child who was always asking questions, soaking up knowledge like a luffa. But when Daedalus lost the queen's favor and they were imprisoned in the tower, Daedalus closed himself off, and Icarus's queries tapered; the fountain of curiosity was extinguished, and rust and residue closed it to the future. In his mind's eye Daedalus looked tenderly at his son and saw the darkness that framed him, the darkness of walking through long unlit corridors, knowing the way but still feeling the wall for comfort, for affirmation from a cold stone that a physical world still existed and yet was not too close and not too dangerous, that it would guide but not disappear and not attack. The darkness between where he had been and where he wanted to be. The unknown between an old comfort and a new one. Every memory of Icarus as a boy was clouded, and Daedalus knew why. The father had always been looking ahead or above, never down towards the child looking up at him. Too late Daedalus understood that any god worth worshipping was after the heart.

The rose-glow of dawn tinted the crying eye of the world on the distant horizon, and Daedalus rubbed his sleepless eyes. He sat up, but moved no further. He watched the sunrise silently. Once Daedalus had almost believed the sun would bow to him, but in the mere hours after liberation from his prison he saw that the sun was ambivalent: neither good nor evil, neither powerful nor weak, neither rewarding nor punishing. But still so much more than he was. Still shining, still rising and setting and feeding the earth, when he was weakest of all days. The kind of faithfulness with which he might be wooed to hope.

The first few nights after the accident he had prostrated himself on the sand and wept in despair. He thought of every transgression he had ever committed, and he repented of them all, over and over again. He prayed emotive and desperate prayers. He thought of every invention he had ever made. They were all so much refuse. The gentle waves lapped his fingertips, stretched out towards he knew not what. The days passed. Over time he began to sit up.

At one point he laughed.

When Daedalus had still been favored in Crete, the queen had manipulated him into crafting the machine that would birth the Minotaur by insinuating that Icarus would suffer if Daedalus refused. Of course, Daedalus was already tempted to do it because of the promise of glory that would come from executing such an impossible feat. But would the queen have used his son as collateral if she had not believed what even Daedalus was too dull to see? That despite his jealous, corrupted, vainglorious heart, he loved his son.

Autumn was coming on, and the sun warmed his toes as it crept up over the horizon. It felt like a betrayal to receive it, but the betrayal had already occurred, and so he stayed. Daedalus felt tired, but the old seaman would be along soon, and he could see it would be a good day for fishing. Porpoises swam by with no audience to watch their majestic backs rise and dive except one wretched wanderer. Sea turtles waddled by him with no care than they would give to a bleached shard of shell. The song of nereids drifted across the water, and it was a song of mercy. From somewhere deep in memory came the words to an old hymn for the old man of the sea, one unerring and gentle, true and just, who knows when to say enough. *Oh that I should live to become half such a man.* Those long-forgotten words came now: a hymn for a god whose name Daedalus had once known.

Over the summer Daedalus had begun to accept the sun's warmth and his own need for it, and he had found comfort in the salt of the never-ending waves. Slowly he had gained a sense of peace that was novel and wonderful like the touch of an infant's skin. The gods would have grace, then.

Daedalus stood up and wiped the sand off his legs, and it glittered like silver in the morning, the morning of grace-again. He returned to his workshop to think for a moment before it was time to take the boat out. When he opened the door, the sunlight illuminated the panels on the sawhorses and the broken remnants of wings in the corner. The fisherman had collected the feathers like they were so many tuna; in his grief Daedalus could not have cared less what happened to them. But the day that he laughed in the barren twilight, Daedalus knew that the broken wings had been saved for a reason.

When the sun was still a quivering yolk on the black pan of the sea, the fisherman arrived, and they dragged the boat down to the water again. In the boat, the two men were silent. From the sea, Daedalus could see a small brown speck on a rocky outcropping far down the beach from the shack. Once the panels were finished, the wings would go inside the rocky shrine and be sealed. The fisherman saw Daedalus's eye stray towards the outcropping. They fished all morning, and after the woman fed them, Daedalus returned to working on the panels.

On the righthand panel were images of things that Daedalus could not be blamed for. There was prince Androgeus, heir of Crete, bleeding from his heart on some distant field. He would never know the bounteous joy of fulfilling the role he was born for, nor the way his death would set off a horrible chain reaction leading to the suffering of so many innocents. Next to him on the wood were the youths who would be sacrificed to the Minotaur, bold and beautiful unfortunate ones. Behind them their parents' faces were punctuated by terror, and before them was the pitcher from which their fate had been drawn.

On the left-hand panel were the worst of the things Daedalus had made: the machine that produced offspring with neither love nor care nor understanding; the babe turned monster, teeth bared and nostrils flared; the labyrinth, directionless and devoid of light, that had shaped him. From left to right, the line of children walked toward the labyrinth gate, which was represented by the break in the two panels. The Minotaur waited in the center of the winding paths that crossed the entire panel, but for one blank space—

Again, Daedalus heard the fisherman's feet softly padding behind him. This time Daedalus did not turn, and they both stood silently appraising the panels. The carvings were not Daedalus's best work. Once he might have been tempted to think so, but no matter how skillfully it is constructed, one does not rejoice at the mausoleum of one's pride. There were errors in the carving. Androgeus's expression showed his pain, but not his anger. Daedalus had made the tributes too young, much younger than the ones who had really died in the Minotaur's lair. The tributes he had carved were so young that they were more afraid of being separated from their mothers than of dying. The faces of their parents in the background were small and less detailed than the children, because Daedalus knew there was no way to accurately depict the fullness of that agony. Or perhaps it was because he did not know what the expression should rightly be. Even the Minotaur did not look quite right. His eyes were too close—that was it—they made him look too human. And then of course, there was the blank corner—the mark of an artist who has poorly planned his canvas. Daedalus's hands itched to turn the wood, to make it beautiful and expressive, but he knew that he could not. *It is mercy,* Daedalus thought. *The signified is greater than the sign itself.*

"The shrine—is it for your son?" the fisherman asked.

They were both looking at the smooth corner of the left-hand panel. *Had the fisherman and his wife ever had children?* Daedalus did not know. Someday, maybe, he would ask. He turned around, wiping the sawdust off his hands, and smiled at the old man wanly.

"For the god of mercy."

In the coming days, Daedalus would finish building the shrine that the panels would decorate. His skills would not go unnoticed by the king of his newfound land, and he would be commissioned to work for him until one day his renown reached too far, too close to the past, and he would renounce that kind of work once and for all. One day he would write to Icarus's mother, who had no way of knowing what had happened to her son. Daedalus would beg for her forgiveness, and she would find her way across the sea to him. One day, far in the future, he would hold her in his arms once more, and look into her eyes, and see there a piece of something that came from no mortal, but which could only be a reflection of the heavens: the age-old sea-grey light of grace. And they would worship at this shrine together.

But those thoughts were not in his mind yet. The new life was now, and grace was now too, new with every sunrise.

Out in the skiff with the quiet old fisherman dragging the nets behind them, Daedalus thought of how the water had cleansed him, though he had not realized that at first.

A few days later when he set the finished panels in place at the shrine, Daedalus made a vow, on the beach that was the threshold of life and death, to honor the true god with every gift he was given, and he ran his hand over the smooth place where his son should have been.

The Way
by Meg Moseman

And to the east I hear that halting song.
The hot steam rises in the winter air.
My raiment—rags; the journey has been long.
Sun and sulfur, rushing. My feet are bare.
On all sides, white. From the mist a wild hare
appears, departs, dun, fleeting, but no tree,
no bird, no hill, no other beast be there.
The way is not yet clear, so follow me.

The many paths are one—they are not wrong,
who teach this, though, itinerant, we share
little enough. The light that hangs among
the water-spouts above the flats is prayer
made visible by steam. The heat's the care
we give each other, while we are not free,
though freedom will erupt, gainsay who dare.
The way is not yet clear, so follow me.

I faint, although once strong as wires are strong.
I have been weeks without the plainest fare,
and to the east I hear that halting song.
The hot steam rises in the winter air.
The dream, the sky, the mud, a white nightmare—
for months there has been nothing more to see.
The dream, the sky, the mud, a hot white prayer—
the way is not yet clear, so follow me.

"the way—is here," he sings, "the way—is there,"
"the way—is hid, the way—is plain to see."
Cracking tenor: "The way is everywhere,
the way—is not yet clear—so—follow me—"

Melody of the Deep
by David Ehrenman

Now Maglina Međuvila wandered into a new land, and hardly had she arrived but messengers came to meet her. They saw a woman's figure below average in height and strikingly powerful. The human vila's face wore knowledge beyond her youth, and experience growing to match it. Over her cloak, hairs white or silver—though not those of age—flowed just below her broad shoulders. Under her arm, the emissaries marked a helm with a wondrous mask. The elder messenger had enough experience to recognize the other war gear beneath Maglina's cloak. For her part, Maglina saw two mounted figures, a slightly hunched woman of many years and a boy hardly younger than herself carrying himself with great pride. Both wore caps on their dark hair and rich garb that spoke of some importance in their rank and purpose. So armed they approached Maglina with intent and stood their horses before her, though they did not dismount.

"Hail, traveler! When we heard of your coming, we knew you for someone both powerful and strange, and marked your arrival in our land. We have heard rumours of you and your haughty bearing, strange language, and rich gear, though you seem not to wear such now." Beside the speaker, the elder messenger frowned at the eagerness bent into an arrogant tone.

"I am indeed a stranger here, as I am in many places, but I do not travel to be asked questions of myself. Rather I seek to hear and learn of you and yours." Bowing on her horse, the elder acknowledged the proud princess and advanced beyond the junior. As she passed, the emissary put out an arm as if moving the inexperienced junior physically aside. The dragon's daughter did not show the hand on her swordhilt.

"Pride breaks through your humble words. But we do not come to interrogate or otherwise waylay you. We come from Hedringa, queen of the Spearings. Some tale of you or your deeds has reached our queen's ear. She has a favor to ask of you, if you prove to be the champion or witch she thinks. For this reason, we ask you to come with us and see her. Forgive the boldness of my junior, for he is young in years and trade."

Maglina nodded and said to the one "Care well for your junior," and to the other, "learn well from your senior. As for your words, they seem good to me. I will come with you and meet your queen. Then we will see if I will tell my name and if my prowess may come to your aid. Go quick ahead of me; let us see who may arrive first. I will find my own way."

So it was that Maglina went on foot even as the messengers rode on horseback, at their side going riderless cantered the swift steed brought for their guest. Even so, when the emissaries returned to the hall of their queen, they found the vila, who bounded as with wings across the heavily wooded land, taking long strides. Long did the memory of even this small deed live on in that queen's court.

In the hall before the monarch, Maglina Međuvila put off her traveling garb. At the foot of the wooden dais testifying the queen's wealth, the wanderer stood in sparse but glorious war gear. On her shoulders, broad as a bear's, folded magnificent spaulders that ran down to her elbows in lames unfurling like wings. No wonder it was said in the land of the Spearings that Maglina Međuvila was a falcon. But in the hall's glow, the armor sheer and barely glinting seemed like scales, the shield her guardian wore. She bore the helm carved about with marvelous scenes and presented herself to the queen through the dread mask. The interlace upon the mask wore not the form of wyrms, but, writhen in a mystery, the raveled script revealed prophecies to fairy folk and seers. To any and all who meet the dragon's foster-child in battle, the frozen face assures the foretelling will be soon fulfilled, the coming of their death. More silent, more hollow the void of the gold lips that mirrored Maglina's mouth. Above the dark wide eyes, gold wings spread like a feathered set of brows. Openly she stood with the Dragon's Tooth, that magical blade, on her side. Before Maglina, arrayed with the handiwork of the Hidden Kingdom's fairies, even the queen seemed poor despite her belt of golden thread and neck adorned by jewels.

"Your majesty, humble I come before you. What help do you seek? I tell you, if it is within my power I will do it."

The queen looked on Maglina Međuvila with haughty eyes set in her shapely face. She sat tall and offered the kneeling warrior no grace but her attention. Vainly did the king to her right seek to catch his sovereign's eyes as he reached across to touch the hand gripping the throne's wood arm.

"Welcome to the hall of Hedringa, queen of the Spearings. Who are you, who receives this hall's hospitality?"

"I am honored by your invitation and your kindness, your majesty. I am Maglina Međuvila."

"You are named Međuvila?" The king's eyes grew bright and he leaned forward in his seat, for he was great in lore and knew more than rumors of the Hidden Folk, even hearing of the vila, Maglina's foster-mother. Before the princess could answer, though, the queen spoke again.

"Though you do not tell much, the whispers and your gear testify you do know something of magic and the hidden powers of the world. It is for this that I grant you audience and offer you the chance at great renown, and gifts" Hedringa paused a moment, as if waiting for Maglina to say something, but the princess stood resolute and silent. The mouth behind the mouth stayed closed. Taking the opportunity, the king spoke instead.

"Our only daughter is lost to us and we do not know what has become of her. Dear Atheldryde, known for her wisdom in this land and many others, with a voice working miracles and magic,"

"Atheldryde, our daughter, beloved of the Spearings, is held captive by an evil power in a labyrinth underneath the Wildren Moors."

Too eager, the king broke in and continued: "The labyrinth is the work of ancient giants, but long ago became haunted by the spirits on the moors. Alone they are troublesome, but gathered all together they grow into something truly terrible. They reached out from the labyrinth and waylaid any who wandered the moors, driving people mad or simply taking them for some purpose untold. An entire league of sorcerers gathered together before we could reclaim any of that country for the Spearings, and even then it was long before they succeeded in reaching the labyrinth and sinking it beneath the ground." With a look of tolerant annoyance, the queen permitted so much before speaking again.

"The best of the Spearings enter the labyrinth only with their ears plugged firmly so they might not go mad, but even so none go far before the power remaining in the maze drives them out with unbearable fury. The wizards, also, sent by my husband return defeated. However, you, I think, may have both might and magic. So I ask you if you will seek Atheldryde and bring her back to Hedringa's hall. If you do so, you may be rewarded unlike any living champion. In gear and rings, in land and jewels, even to the hand of beautiful Atheldryde, much may be yours if you succeed."

"And we offer all you may require to accomplish it. Supplies and companions you shall not lack when you do this," added the king.

"I thank you for your hospitality. I will seek out the labyrinth and discover your princess, if I may." Saying no more, Maglina turned and walked out of the hall.

Maglina entered the labyrinth unafraid of the ghostly sound that rang the doorway. Though there was no door, the entrance rang thick with vibrations sturdier than wood. The magic resisted her, even though her ears under the heavy helm were plugged up with leaves as she had been warned. Farther in Maglina moved, with no regard for which way she wove like a spider after the patterned web another made. Still the sound moved, the ripples of that other spider reaching out through aural threads forming an extension of itself, and a prison for any other. Despite her guard, Maglina Meðuvila heard discordant tones so strong and wrong the leaves bled clear and drops fell in her ears and down her neck. Maglina thought of her mother, remembering the water of her lake lingering on her skin when she emerged to land again. No indication pointed down one way or another, from or toward the source, the labyrinth's beating heart, and the monster pumping venom out. Out from her ears Maglina tore the futile leaves and left them lying, drying out beside the mosses' other greens for company, and by the stone stained brown with running water. On her side she hefted the helm; bareheaded and unmasked, the child of mists confronted the labyrinth anew, unaided. And so she found a miracle: the sound changed into something like to music.

After so long a separation from the fairies of the Hidden Kingdom, her ears but slowly recognized the similarity between their songs and the tunes emerging from the maze, appearing now as their true selves to ears that knew and understood them. Before Maglina only heard noise, but now she heard no cacophony–this was haunting rather than horrible. Sharply and sweetly the notes caressed her hand and carved emotions on her heart in musical runes. Notes sounded from a throat, and deeper from a belly, then again yet deeper from the underworld of wisdom and memory and imagination. Other musical phrases laid frost on the moss and grass, and braided hair as long as ages. From it all, the playful and the narrative, Maglina heard one heart: a joy poured into music. She found the joy to be deep, the kind that flows from a spring knowing suffering. Among the myriad melodies and interweaving harmonies, the dragon's daughter slowly clarified the way as she pressed her ear to the wall. The music led her on by guiding steps felt through her feet engrossing nearly all attention. For the rest, she marveled at the songs changing in each new hall as each new branching choice drew her closer to the heart. Some doorways welcomed, gladly open, smooth in sounding shifts. Others seemed disjointed, offering a part of the resistance that the vila's daughter felt when first she entered, and the two sides held different songs. Armed with senses trained among the fairy folk, Maglina thought of stars and knew the voice breathed long life into their music. Each change came not from a moment's whim but years of spinning songs that wandered as instructed or inclined–that much Maglina could not tell—about the labyrinth.

Long enough to sleep twice in chambers full of lullabies the child of mists kept on about the mazy paths. Where the sound waves formerly pushed her to the edge of their world and out of it, now they pulled her in to the deep most beautiful and terrible, and more than these, immeasurable. And at last she found a hall she did not need to light. Stone and roots as old as Earth built out the walls and roof all rounded in the manner she had seen the fairies dwelling deep in the mountains cut their treasured jewels for little elves to take as homes. Like those, the cavern's shape reflected light inside, and not from without. No clever hands and no tools had shaped this place, however; the music in its power worked it all. There, in the center of the floor, she saw the maze's heart.

Two figures stood there. One was a great creature in nearly the shape of a bear or a dragon, though several times larger than either. From its back, what looked like branches or roots sprouted and reached like a hand to hold the fireflies glowing yellow-green that gathered in the manner of moths about the creature. Its fur looked similar to a brushed cat's, or cut grass, though twice as long. Blind white eyes glinted green and silver in a gentle face holding strong through years legibly written on it. There before its face and facing it stood the figure of a human woman. Maglina knew her in an instant for the princess, but saw in her a star nearly as bright as heaven. The vila saw Atheldryde full of light and closer than the sun, sparkling and flaring with a beauty she could study like the face of the moon. In that moment, Maglina learned distrust in human quests.

Over and under their continuing song, a two-toned voice spoke in welcome's spirit: "Our music told us now you've come."

"It is good to feel at home," the dragon's child replied, nearly to herself, as she looked around with a combination of familiarity and wonder.

"Glad we are to hear it," the voice laughed like the rush of a waterfall. Seeing the labyrinth so thoroughly theirs, Maglina knew their choice to stay and saw the healing of a heart split long ago. The princess recognized the single presence of the Voice, the Melody in the deep, and knew she would not ask about Atheldryde, though she might learn what she could from the Voice, or if she caught some wisp of the story floating about the maze.

"I am a child of Mists, and it has been long since I walked in the Hidden Kingdom, hearing its music. I delight to meet you and wish to know you."

"If you are of the Hidden Kingdom, do you know the dragon?"

"I am their daughter," Maglina said.

The voice wailed, the labyrinth wailed. The voice screamed, the maze screamed. Nearly the howl drove the vila from the cavern, but Maglina kept her resolute heart. Water, blood, and sap poured from the walls until the floor was flooded, rising up to the daughter's knees. Back bent sound waves long ago cried from the heart, and one tone began to mourn like creatures long dead while another tone cursed the dragons. Then they told Maglina of a home that was forgotten.

> Humanity hellbent and careless
> Serpentine desperate and hungry
> Umani slaughtered and eaten
> Blood drops and tear stains
> Silence   Silence

Through her strength of spirit, still Maglina stood against the horrors resurrected, a past roused from long rest underneath a hard-forged peace. When at last the fury's worst subsided, as she stood nearly drowning in the flood now above her neck, the dragon's daughter spoke.

> Love leaves grief as loss's remnant,
> Ghosts are wrought from grief. So
> We know that ghosts are made of love
> For treasured memory in company to life.

> Here I am –   I'll hold you
> If you wish   or bear your curse.
> As I live   the Hidden Kingdom
> Guiltless stands,   or, guilty, falls
> With me.   There is home
> In a prison   or an exile land,
> There is hope   for the mourning
> For a moment   take my hand
> And in this place   now take my life.

No frothing anger crested the waves of terrible pain crashing down on Međuvila. The voice in the deep Maglina heard, and through the sound, it made a space for the take her. Commanded by the melody, even the flood parted so that the vila stood like a sapling in its well.

"Tell us yourself, and we will take you. We will take your life." So told Maglina Međuvila of her life begun as an orphan in the girdling mist, found by gentle fairies and presented to the dragon. Full she told them of the banquet celebrating as the Hidden Power chose her for their daughter, and the years spent by the mountain lake in trust of the motherly vila tending. Spoke the daughter of the dragon's teaching, and her leaving, then her journeys leading here. As she spun her life in song, the voice of the labyrinth's heart began to change, and wordless, harmonized her tone.

"This life we take, and we will sing. We thank you for your gift surrendered willingly. We see the resonance of home that echoes in this cavern. Glad we are to hear you now and glad we are to find a friend." Through this answer peace was forged between Maglina and the voice. History passed and judgment too. Steady beats the maze's heart again, and back flowed out the blood to feed the labyrinth's body.

"Tell me of your home," Maglina said again. She heard a home indeed.

"The sanctuary guards and changes us, it comforts us into ourselves. Here we search ourselves and find the Earth."

"Speak to us of fairy folk, dear child." Then the human vila told of stories, all the fairies with their clever hands and winding paths. By itself the song of welcome in response pushed back the remnant flood and warmed the child of mists as much as any embrace a princess and Umani might have given long ago, long before they stood transformed and rooted. After welcome, back they turned to songs they chose, and seemed to forget the presence of their visitor. Round Maglina wove the musical threads unwrapping tales of otherworlds or simple hearts and wrapping wisdom closely kept by the depths of the Earth. Where above, she might have lived a week, or a month, the dragon's daughter sat her down and nearly lost herself to the voice, the melody in the Deep. But at last Maglina rose and took her leave. The princess found, the music heard, the voice at home, the Child of Mists went out the labyrinth to venture once again through human lands, and others.

At the edge of the overworld, back she sang:

Make memory imagination,
One become another.
Rest gave birth to joy and wisdom shared
With me, an other.

Deep of earth and air you'll drink,
Let fly your ringing songs.
Live long and dwell here in your peace and
Keep your heartbeat strong.

Maglina walked over the moors toward the highlands. She did not return to Hedringa's hall for she would not reveal, nor would she cover, the secret of the labyrinth to those who saw it for a prison.

Grandmother Anna

By Kenneth Burtness

I was scared of a lot of things when I was young, but I was never really afraid of dying. My grandmother Anna protected me with a ferocity that no one living or dead could face. Anna was 25 when she died shortly after giving birth to my Uncle Kip, leaving my Aunt Carol, two years old, and my father, four years old, with my grandfather, Henry, a roughhewn immigrant farmer.

She could not believe the Gods had taken her away from her young children and kept her from nurturing them as they grew. So she stayed and forged a sword out of her anger. Woe be to anyone who threatened her three children.

They say Anna was beautiful with a smile and a voice that could soften the most obstinate and coax a laugh from the most serious, but I only saw her angry dead face once. I was having a terrifying dream and I startled awake. She was standing by my bed looking down at me, her long red hair streaming behind her like fire in the wind. I saw her hard face slowly relax into a gentle loving smile. Though her lips moved not, I clearly heard her say she would protect me. Then she turned and walked away, and I returned easy to my slumber.

Her sword was now protecting her grandchildren, of whom I was the first. When I was falling asleep at night, I could hear the howling of Monsters and catch glimpses of the Dead flying around outside. But I could also see my grandmother's back as she stood at my window looking out, watching, her sword in her hand at the ready, old blood encrusted on its edges.

Now she stands by the window of my two grandsons. On dark nights when the wind is wild and dark things roam, I know she is in their room, the moon illuminating her bloody sword, striking fear in any evil creature who has ventured too close.

If the moans and lamentations of the uneasy dead wake my grandsons, and if they fail to see their great-great-grandmother at their window guarding them, and run from their room, that is okay. For Anna knows as I do that they have run into my daughter's room to burrow under the covers with her and my son-in-law.

Then I believe Anna's back muscles relax slightly, for my daughter is a fearsome protector as well. And I remember once more the gentle loving smile of my sword-wielding grandmother.

Dragon's Rest
by Daniel J. Pool

Gilclaw was tired. His hands ached. His knees creaked. The dragon had outlived his hoard and now he was all but waiting to die. The thrill of hunting had left him. His senses dulled by time enjoyed luxury no longer. Now the herds did not run from him. The goats and sheep of the rolling hills would graze around him when he slept in the prairie grass. Wymlings had already begun pushing into his territory. Though masterless, they saw the elder not as someone to respect but as washed-up. Barely worth the carrion to hunt.

The ancient green dragon had been fearsome once. When he reached adulthood, he auditioned for a particularly ruthless red dragon lord for his pilgrimage. His master was good to him and taught him the ways of war. When he was ready, he had taken mortal form and begun a campaign of conquest. The pilgrimage was meant to humble dragons with knowledge of humanity. However, like most dragons of that age, it was a time to gather their hoard of wealth.

For dragonkin, the hoard was more than gold and jewels, though. This collection represented their rank in life and the afterlife. Dragon faith took the accumulation of wealth to represent their worth. To outlive one's hoard meant a dragon was either a poor provider or lazy. In Gilclaw's case, there had been a particularly dire famine. The fallout from a neighboring war had chilled the land from which the dragon needed to plunder. When the soil and its people had healed, Gilclaw's best years were already behind him. He had spent those dark times helping the people instead of slaying them.

He had lived simply. Made the gold he had earned last as long as possible. By the time he had run out, he was too old to audition like a wyrmling again. His only hope was to pass from combat. A warrior's death could buy him the grace he lacked gold to purchase. The warriors no longer told tales of his strength. The herders no longer feared his bite. No adventurers would travel to the valley to fight where there was no glory.

When Gilclaw had grown so tired that he no longer feared crossing the star bridge, he made a plan. There was a girl known to him in the village of Hogford in the next valley who sought to become an adventurer. Despite several years of naysaying by her parents, she had never relented in her goal. When her chores at home were done and the flock grazing safely, the girl would practice with a wooden sword she had found. She had been so pleased to find the exact item she needed to learn her desired craft that she never questioned where it had come from. Gilclaw had overheard her wish while in the form of a beggar. She had told him while giving him a crust of bread. The act reminded him why he had chosen a life of poverty instead of wanton bloodshed for his gain.

The only place to safely perform her forms was in Gilclaw's Valley. Her parents told her it was too dangerous, but she knew the ancient dragon was gentle. Every day she could, she went to the valley and practiced with the sword. When she was proficient with the sword, a shield appeared. When she mastered the shield, a bow and arrow appeared. And when she had mastered the bow, a steel sword appeared. She was hesitant to accept this gift, however. No one else came to this place save for the lumpy scaley hill snoring in the grass. So, the girl marched up to the dragon and kneeled before his snout. She waited for him to wake because he was asleep, and she was polite. When that took more time than she thought was appropriate, she plucked a feather from the ground and tickled his nose with it. He woke with a start and a sneeze.

"Fear me mortal! How dare you wake me from my slumber! I shall dash your blood upon the rocks!" Gilclaw said with his most convincing angry voice.

The girl stared at him in quiet annoyance.

"Fear me, Edith!"

"I didn't tell you my name, Mr. Gilclaw. And don't think me a fool. Why did you leave this weapon for me?"

The dragon snarled at the little girl. He raked his claws on a nearby boulder. Green flames snapped from his jaw. The small villager only looked at the creature with an annoyed pout. The dragon huffed when he saw this ploy was not having the intended effect.

"Fine," said Gilclaw. "You win. I want a warrior's death. I've outlived my hoard, brood, friends, mates, and purpose. Only dying in combat could grant me access to the Golden Hunting Grounds."

"But I am no warrior. I could find someone to help. Or maybe I could hire a traveling adventurer."

The dragon shook its head slowly accompanied by several pops and cracks from his stiff neck. Gilclaw said, "There is no time now for finding someone. Besides, you are the most skilled warrior in the valley." He motioned his snout toward the archery range she had practiced at as well as the tree she had practiced her swordplay on. "I have faced many fighters in my years. You will be great among them."

Edith smiled but the light in her eyes drained. She said, "I wish my mother or father would agree. They don't think there is much to do beyond herding and sewing."

"Herding and mending are honorable trades. You will be wonderful at anything you set your mind to. However, you took to the ways of war quicker than most men I trained in my youth. If only there were some terrible threats to your village. If only some great danger could arise in which you could show your talent. Then your parents would be forced to accept your wishes."

The girl chewed on these words and then said, "Some terrible threat… Like, say a dragon attack?"

Gilclaw looked hurt. He held a wing to wipe an invisible tear. "You already struck me, mortal, with a deadly assault upon my character. Such brutal words. Then again… If that were to happen, it is good you have trained yourself. I would wager you could save the village if a dragon were to attack."

Edith asked, "Is that a threat?"

The dragon shouted, "Your village is as far as I can travel. Any further and I would surely die of natural causes. You are the only villager with the courage to face me. Anyone else would falter. This is not a threat but rather the truth of the world. If I am to reach the vaulted heavens, my only choice is to attack your kith and kin."

"But I am so small yet. I don't have the strength to drive a sword or arrow through your scales."

Gilclaw smiled. He pushed himself off the ground with his front legs. Taking one long talon, he pointed to a place on his chest. A scar decades-old but still glistening. The armored scales had never regrown over the spot. The girl nodded solemnly.

Edith said, "But I am too young. Is it possible for you to wait till I'm old enough to fight you as an adult?"

Gilclaw snorted, "Adventure does not call upon you when it is convenient and neither do I. If I waited till you were of age, I would be bones. Damned to an eternity of pain in the hells of cowards. I want you to fight me and honor your wish to yourself. I want to give one last hero a story to build their legacy on."

"Will anyone get hurt?"

The dragon cocked his head to the side before returning to the ground. He looked at her with his bright yellow eye. Gilclaw said, "I certainly hope so at least for my sake. However, I will attempt to avoid gratuitous destruction. You should know though; it is often said one should never make a bargain with a dragon."

Edith said, "Because you can't trust dragons?"

"No, because dragons always tell the truth but serve their own desires above others." The dragon's eyes had begun to droop. "Lucky for you, what I want is to die with honor." Gilclaw nuzzled his head against the soft grass. "One last glorious fight. One last grand adventure."

With that exchange, Gilclaw settled back into snoring and Edith left for home. The late summer sun was already growing cold. It had begun to dip toward the horizon. She herded the sheep while she tried to steel her nerves. This is what she wanted. Now that adventure had come to her, however, she was unsure she wanted the burden of what she had wished for. What if the other villagers got hurt? What if the whole town burned down? She would never forgive herself if that happened. So, she decided, she must prepare even more till the day comes.

The green dragon did not appear the next day. Or the day after. For two weeks, there was no sign of the dragon at all. Edith did not falter but trained harder. She began to wake early to exercise and practice with her sword. When she walked through the village, she made mental notes about where she could climb, hide, and run in the event of a dragon attack. The village was not a fortress and years of peace had enforced this philosophy in its construction. Thatched roofs, timber walls, and multi-family homes scrunched together in tight pockets. A dragon attack would burn most of their homes.

Edith decided to create an arena to fight Gilclaw. Knowing he would want to fight on the ground, she set a trap for him. Her parents had a barn near their home they used to winter their flocks. The fenced yard in front of it had been used to help separate them during shearing season. So it was already relatively open with heavy wooden rails to help keep the stubborn sheep from running away. Between this yard and the corrals, she could force the dragon to fight her on her terms. When her parents were not watching, she dug trenches and covered them with sticks, hay, and mud. Strong enough to support a human or a sheep but not a dragon's claw. Lastly, she drove a timber into the middle of the yard. She claimed she was going to help break a colt in with a friend but kept the details of the colt and friend quiet. As if it was nothing too important. Her parents thought she had finally come around to continuing the family's agrarian lifestyle.

They learned just how wrong they were a few days later when the ancient green dragon landed in the yard to inspect a trio of sickly sheep Edith had suspiciously tied to the Patience Pole. She told her parents that they would need to be treated or slaughtered soon. They did not suspect that she had rubbed fresh pigs' blood from the butcher shop into their wool to attract the beast. Gilclaw landed with a hefty wheeze and began to pick at the prepared meal.

Edith had been waiting. She did not, however, rush the dragon with a sword and shield. This he had expected. Instead, she released D'Artagnan, the family herding dog. The massive mutt was either born too proud or had been headbutted too many times by rams to know it was outmatched. Harsh barking filled the air and made the old wyrm recoil defensively. Gilclaw snapped one of the elderly sheep up in one bite then crouched preparing to snatch the dog too. Then the arrows began pelting him. They struck his head and wings. Irritated, he tried to position himself equidistant from both dog and archer. The dragon, however, had been maneuvered much like his snack directly into a series of shallow spike-filled pits. He released a coarse roar that shook the barn and rattled Edith to her bones.

This was the signal. From the hay loft, the young warrior swung out on a rope onto the creature's back. Between the cacophony of barking, the pain in his paws, and now a human riding his back, Gilclaw was becoming angry. His brain was on fire with the audacity of the attack. Rage surged through him. He intended to kill this girl now. He did not have long to meditate on this hate. Edith threw a rope around his neck. This was the last straw for the dragon. A fight was one thing, even one with traps. But ridding a dragon of his esteem was an insult. He thought maybe she had the wrong idea about this fight. Just to show her how cruel he could be, he snapped his head around to bite her at a twisting angle.

This was, unfortunately for Gilclaw, exactly what Edith wanted. She threw the last of the rope around his snout and rapelled to the ground. She tied off the rope to the Patience Pole. Unlike for horses, she had used the longest pole she could barter for and weighed it down before burying it. Now the dragon was stuck in an uncomfortable position and having trouble freeing himself. With his neck bent backward and twisted, he could not summon the strength to break the heavy cables.

The girl withdrew the sword the dragon had given her from a stack of hay. She laid a hand on the scar where his scales had never grown back. He held her gaze with the one massive eye he could manage to face toward her. Then Edith plunged the sword deep into Gilclaw's heart. Thick green blood oozed from the wound and soaked the entire pen. The mud turned instantly to thick carpets of grass and flowers blooming as his heart pumped its last back into the land he had watched over for hundreds of years.

She pressed her head to his neck and whispered, "Thank you."

He did not say anything directly, but she felt his tense muscles relax as he settled into death. His bright yellow eye slowly glazed and closed one last time. The wyrm almost looked to be sleeping once more as he had looked for hundreds of years.

The people of Hogford praised Edith. She became their champion. In time, she even became the adventurer she had dreamed of becoming. What she never did, however, was forget the gentle green dragon. She wore one of his fangs till the day she fought her last battle. But that was a story for another time.

Wee Beastie, by Phillip Fitzsimmons

Echo Still

by Jon Heggestad

Three pining figures curl around the lip of the pool in various states of decay. The remnant of the man above is the most obvious. Although his skin has tapered down, sucked hollow, what survives remains brilliant. The makings of an Adonis still shines through.

Shining, too, is the gleam in his hair. The wind, in all its admiration, has combed it through, sweeping it back in a wish to breathe new life.

Shining, too, is the glint of his eyes, both soft and intense in their downward gaze. Somewhere out of sight, a band of birds rings loudly and often as they pay service to this, their favorite, tableau.

Shining, too, is the man below, a twin to the man above in every way. Even in death, beauty calls out to beauty. They bend over the pond's edge, both constant and confident, in their mutual adoration.

A leaf drifts down between the men and disturbs the thin layer that separates them. The birds, which had just now been speaking of the figures, fall suddenly silent, annoyed at the disturbance. Yet, and perhaps in reassurance, the man below winks slowly, the movement traveling down the length of his body in a ripple of flirtation—unmatched but nevertheless appreciated by not only the man above but the flock still higher.

The third figure in this set is more difficult to make out; there is so little of her that remains. She is nothing more, really, than a pair of lips, still poised just behind the left ear of the man above. From a different angle, the lips above might find a likeness of their own in the pond's depths, appearing behind the ear—the right ear, that is—of the man below.

It's the wrong angle, perhaps, or a trick of the light, for the lips are only here. They are only visible behind this, less liquid, left ear.

As the twins remain lovely despite the sallow, sunken aging of their corpses, the pair of lips continues warm, full, and inviting despite their strange isolation.

A cupid's bow dips low into a divot, nestling deep into the oval lower lip while the dark corners of the mouth slant upward in a quiet plea. The angle, too, holds a hint of old laughter, reinforced by the restless dimple residing just beneath this arc.

A rustle in the treetops above the pond stirs the slow but steady heartbeat of the three figures. A strand of hair threads its way off the sallow skin of the twins' brows, blown back into the rivulets of wavy curls that descends down their napes, their necks. The strand above shifts against the pair of lips, which peel apart, a quick intake of breath. Like a band with its tension suddenly released, they snap into a momentary, unintended O. With more deliberation, they stretch themselves thin. They curl up, then down, and then, they speak.

As I told Iris, deep in the woods, somewhere between our neighboring trees, I'd never seen a man so handsome, never in all my life. I said the trees went still. I said the birds sang out. I said the foxes stopped and waited, sitting patiently in the grass to watch you as you walked. I said they sit so close, so eager to see you, that their coats would brush your feet. I told her your laughter cooed around them, how they sprawled across your happy wake.

Iris laughed. She said that beauty was a path to nowhere. She chided me. She said I'd followed foxes too many times before. I said it's not the same. She said it's all the same. She said the only change was the one she hoped I'd find.

Then, finding fair Iris, I told her what I'd seen. I said I'd watched you from afar. I said I'd prove her wrong about you, about me. I said I'd found you beautiful, yes, but also gentle. I asked what man but you would take his time like this, to pause at every flower in his path. I told her how you knew them all by name, how you would call upon them—each and all. I told her how you'd found one so young it hadn't found a name, how you'd whispered "borrow mine" into its trumpet ear, how the blossom flushed to hear it. I told her how you laid it in your peaceful, waiting hand. It bloomed brighter still in the caress of your voice, your gaze and care. I said that you were loving, yes, as well as loved.

Iris laughed. She said that such a pretty flower is wont to grow in groves. She circled all around her, pointing out a million lesser growths. She chided me. She said to take pride in another's luck that also was your own amounts to nothing, less than nothing. She said to let flowers alone.

I told Iris, later still, your beauty was unearthly sweet. I said that every towering tree bent low to keep you near them, laying fruits down at your feet. I told her you were nearly bruised by peaches tossed too greedily. Fig trees, I said, swung limbs in greeting, hoping for a greeting back, hoping you'd accept their gifts and to stop along your path. I said I'd seen an entire grove work hastily to make a bed of pomegranate seeds. I said I'd never seen you want for anything but these green gifts. I asked what man but you could live so well on nothing but the juice squeezed so lovingly from the fruits of all these trees. I asked what man but you could be so simple, happy, sweet.

Iris laughed. A man can spoil, she waved her hand, a man can come to rot. She said sweetness lasts a season, and a season ends like that. She snapped her fingers. She looked at me until I blushed. She sighed. She said to pine for something stronger, for something that might last.

I found Iris late one night. I bent down and whispered in her ear. I said I'd be yours, and you'd be mine. I told her soon, it would be soon. I laughed at my own words, delighted as I was.

Iris frowned. She took my hand and told me not to rush. She said not to give up so entirely. She pressed her finger against my lower lip, or just the spot below it. She watched my eyes. I blushed again. I couldn't help but smile; I told her so. A crease came down across her gaze.

She said that I was more than this single thought. She said I wouldn't succeed in what I'd said I'd do. She said I was not, am not singular. She said, try as I might, I couldn't give myself away. She said that others held pieces, too. She said she'd never give away this piece she had of me.

I laughed. I chided back. I teased, if worst comes to worst, that I loved an unrequited love all the same.

She told me I'd pronounced it wrong. She said it's not quite *but* quit. *I told her that would be our joke. How, I said, I didn't know, after all, what it was exactly that I was saying. I laughed. I turned away. I was tired of waiting. The joke is, I know, that I was already so tired of waiting.*

Iris watched me go. She called me back, an unrequited calling. Echo, she said—she watched, she waited—it isn't very good, is it, not a good joke at all.

The lips say all of this, a message pre-recorded. They pause, parted, now a gentler O. A brush of hair, an intake of breath, a moment's lull again—this all occurs before a single bird can crow.

But now, the wind, which has patiently listened to this monologue, decides to recommence, and the strand of hair it had earlier played with is once more tossed aside in playful abandon.

With gentle determination, the corners of the mouth peak up and outward.

"A good joke," they repeat, but the small echo is swallowed up by the rest of this quiet forest.

The Stone Circle
at Avebury, England
by Dave Shortt

these feelings were meant to last
thousands of years

beginning to erode
from the curiosity of onlookers,
the sarsens themselves are huge loves, set in
'the sands of time,' silica bonds
of conjugal acts

this object is the potential of fear,
this one is love's potential:
from here,
the burial goods were pillaged,
from here
they'll be left untouched

slowly faith awakens
without caffeine or tobacco,
where leisurely & imaginal works
are created from adrenaline & fire

but if the feeling begins to fade,
cut flowers or a candle's flame
placed in a nearby passage grave
are like a galaxy or star cluster,
reminders of yesterdays

that've expanded & floated
off like vows

& as she finds herself
lying on a nearby barrow as on a bed:
giving birth to the latest generation
whose teeth might all be documented
could be any parent's dream

crowds interweave with the stones,
leaving behind impressions
of their humanity,
made as going-away presents by
a timeless attraction they feel
to overcome, yet stay
in the unique rest mass of
a body encompassing
one & all

their young in brazen skepticism
skip in & out through a huge
'O' of illiteracy as she follows, wanting
to show them how to read
under that vowelless menhir the moon,
whose light propagates in high clouds
an unbroken ripple of her times

Watermill Cove
by Ella Walsworth-Bell

Steve is up to the elbows in flour, fingertips sticky with dough. He pauses for a moment to stare at blue skies through a small high window in the kitchen. The fan blares hot air in his ear, relentless as tides. The radio is playing "Holiday" by Madonna and he's already wondering if he can get away early from this shift. His long hair is caught in a ponytail, and his swim muscles are kneading, kneading dough. The ovens are on as hot as they can go and he's thinking of the coolness of the sea.

"Names," Fliss calls through from the kitchen. "What we gonna call these pizzas, dude?"

He spins the dough on his fingers, stretching lightly until it is a disc, wide and round as this damn island. He imagines the crust bubbling and blistering with heat, like his own burnt-out heart.

"Watermill," he says.

"Is that for the pepperoni? Or the fish one?"

"Nah." He hesitates, holding the space, making her wait. Teasing and twisting another ball of dough in his hands. Watermill Cove is his favorite beach here. There are tall Monterey pines at the top of the hill and a slow steady walk along a lush ferny track to the sea. Boulders, pebbles and finally hard white sand. Untouched. Most people talk about Watermill, but they can't be bothered to walk there. It feels like his own private beach. He half-closes his eyes. Tonight, it'll be all his. When everyone else is sleeping and the next shift doesn't start until eleven. Perhaps he'll even sleep there, curled in the lee of a rock, waiting for seals to haul out and sing at dawn. Perhaps...

Her voice cuts into his daydreams. "So, which one? C'mon, Steve, you're killing me."

"Margherita."

She sticks her head around the door. He stares out the window again.

"Watermill for Margherita," he repeats. "Pelistry for Four Cheese, Porth-humpin' Cressa for your one with the fish, and...Old Town. Veggie option."

She scribbles the names down. "Ta. I'll do the rest."

His heart gives another lurch as she retreats back to the tills. The smell of pizza brings back happy memories—both of them stirring their first batch of tomato sauce, hands entwined around the wooden spoon. He helped her get those recipes exactly right. They worked all winter on the restaurant. And then, the moment they opened, she shacked up with that smarmy git Jonno. The fisherman.

If I weren't strapped for cash, he thinks, *if I hadn't put body and soul into this place, well, I wouldn't be still here, doing her grunt work, would I?* Perhaps it was always about the pizza place. Her first love. Not him.

He takes it out on the dough, screwing it into a ball. Pounds, thumps, shoves it onto the work surface. This is going to be a hell of a summer, working here.

He reaches for the radio and twists the dial up to max. Madonna's voice fills the room. A bead of sweat trickles down his back. *Pretend she's not here. Just make the pizzas, Steve. Get the dough sorted, before the orders come in. Then get down to the beach.* Yeah, he could do this. Easy.

End of the shift and the oven's finally out of fire. The last boxes have been filled, the last of the mozzarella used up. Grated creamy whiteness over all those Watermills and Pelistrys and whatever the hell else they'd named the bloody things. "Need more mozzarella for next time," Steve said, pressing the fridge door closed. He reached for a rag from a plastic tub by the sink and rinsed it under the cold tap to wipe down the work surfaces one by one. Dough sticks: if you don't wipe it away, it's concrete in the morning.

"Wassat?" The noise of coins being counted next to the till stopped dead. "Whatcha need more of?" Fliss stuck her head round the door again, all creased brows and messy hair.

"Mozzarella. Only one left."

"Alright. Delivery boat coming in tomorrow, innit?"

He stopped wiping. Hauled the window shut. "I'll be off, then." Shook his head, knowing where Fliss would be sleeping tonight. Tucked up with Jonno the fisherman. Him with the double pepperoni order and sneaky dark eyes.

Steve closed the back door behind him. "Freaking pizzas," he said, half to himself. The air was warm and smooth as good whiskey. Leaving the alley behind him, he strode past the pub and its lit windows. Likely as not, a few locals would be clustered round a table, finishing their beers. If it'd still been on, with him and Fliss, they'd have gone together, after work. His arm round her shoulders, her eyes staring back at him with the innocence of a kitten.

"Orright, Steve?" Dave the publican draws on a fag.

"Orright, mate." He doesn't break his stride. Fuck the pub, tonight. Fuck them all, because they all bloody knew, *dint they*? About her and Jonno. Whilst he got the pizza place all sorted out for her: skimmed the walls, painted them white, installed the special steel ovens, the lot. All ready for beginning of the season. Their dream restaurant. She'd smiled, lent the odd hand with a brush, and all the while she'd been sneaking off with Jonno behind his back.

So, tonight—he breathed in the fresh air calling him from across Porthcressa bay—tonight, he wasn't going home yet. He'd go for a walk, then a swim. He didn't want to be near anyone else on this island. He paused as he walked along the seafront, staring at the sandy beach. A full moon in a star-bright sky speckled the waves with glossy beams of refracted light. Behind him was the noise and bustle of Hugh Town. He wanted none of that.

Into the side pocket of his chefs' trousers, he'd slipped a bottle. Not fish sauce, this one was special, and his. Whiskey, the good stuff. Perhaps he'd save it for the beach, keep him warm after the swim. Sea water would make everything better. There wasn't no therapy for heartache, here. Swimming—full immersion—that'd do it. Wash off the grime and heat from the oven. There'd be enough nights like this, heat and grime and ovens and Fliss' face, every ten minutes. He needed some kind of help, else he'd go spare.

Steve walked, and walked, and walked some more. Soon he was right out of town, away from the streetlights. The moon cast a long shadow in front of him, and he hesitated where a path led over a stile into the trees. If he took this short cut from nowhere-land into the nature reserve, he'd be half way there in an hour or so. His white plastic chefs' shoes weren't built for these root-torn trails, and so he stopped, necked the whiskey in bitter silence, then kicked them off. Fuck shoes. He'd come back for them in the morning.

The alcohol left a sore taste in his throat, a wanting. Like when he'd looked at Fliss, earlier tonight. He wanted more, but it was all over, wasn't it? The air tasted cooler here, in the semi-darkness under the elder trees. He looked down. Walking here, he'd clenched his fists so tight he'd nipped his fingernails into the hard skin on his palms, drawing blood. Huffing out a sigh, he lobbed the empty glass bottle into one of the pools in the reserve, watching it bob.

"Get in that water, Steve," he muttered to himself.

It wasn't far to Watermill, now. Up the hill, flat feet on tarmac roads without his shoes. It was calm and still on this side of the island. No swell in the bay, no wind in the trees. He strode past Farmer Tom's bulb farm.

Here it was. The path to the cove, even darker than before. These were called the woods, but in reality, they were a scrubby wasteland between fields. Ducks called out a frantic warning at the top of the hill and he swore at them, loud and angry with the alcohol pounding in his veins. Slow clouds swept away the moon's face, blinding him. Right in the darkest heart of this scrubland, on the downwards-sloping muddy path with slippy stones underfoot.

He tripped. Put a hand out, still wet-palmed with his blood.

And there it was. Deep, cool water under his hands, not the ground as he'd imagined.

"What the——?" Off-balance, he lurched sideways: hands, body, face, hair into the water.

Then came the memory: "St. Enwyn's well." He half-breathed, half-said the words. Fliss had brought him here, way back. Ivy curled around the lip of the well and they'd flicked pennies in, wishing for luck. Fliss had said it was ages old, explained that Enwyn wasn't a saint, she was a—what was she, again? A white witch? He lay in the dark night, up to his shoulder in the wishing well.

Leaves rustled, as if there was a breeze. An awakened voice whispered inside his ears as if hushing oceans inside seashells.

Mmmm, you''ve fed me blood. What would you wish for? Tell me, young man.

"Whiskey's talking." A bitter laugh burst forth from his throat. "Prob'ly all in my head." His chefs' trousers were ragged with mud, his feet bruised from walking, his arm muscles tired out from heaving pizza dough around all night.

A wisssshhhhh, the voice hissed.

"Lemme think f'ra min." He closed his eyes and tried to wish for.... oh, he didn't blooming know.

He wished Jonno gone.

Revenge on a love-rival. Nice.

He wished for Fliss.

Are you sure?

"Nah, all I want is a swim." Sod it. He wished for change, is what he wished for.

*Change...*the voice hissed, louder, more insistent...*Change into something that can swim. Give you a tail, and teeth. Hah! You want change, do you?*

"Bugger this for a laugh." Steve heaved himself out of the well. He sat, then stood up. He shook his head so the fresh water droplets span off into the darkness, like a dog. "Hearing voices! Need to clear my head."

He lurched down the path towards the sea. His legs felt awful wobbly. Must be from the long walk. Once he got in the water, he'd be more than fine. He scratched his back: his skin was itching like mad. It felt flaky, scaly, almost like sunburn. Weird, when he'd not been in the sun all week. Nah, he'd been stuck making pizzas, baking pizzas, cleaning kitchens—slaving for Fliss, basically. He scratched again, and something plasticky caught under his fingernail. Pausing, he squinted at it. Looked like a circular piece of packaging. Out of instinct, he sniffed it. Mackerel. Smelt like a fish-scale. His stomach turned and he flicked it into a clump of dark bladderwrack.

"Ugh. Gotta get in."

Once he got his kit off, that cool water would soothe him nicely, wash him off. He was gasping for a swim. In fact, here on this beach he was sucking in great lungsful of fresh sea air and he couldn't breathe straight. His head span as he stripped off his clothes awkwardly, feeling them catch at his skin. Staring at the kaleidoscope of stars, the dizziness hadn't passed. Thinking was slower, colder.

"Oh, stuff this."

Running down the sand, stumbling at the sea, diving headfirst into a luminescent mass of cold ocean. He gaped at the air as he went. It was like nothing was there. His head split in a thump of pain and confusion. His lungs roared. The only thing for it was to stuff himself underwater completely and to stay right there. His hands scrabbled for his neck and here there were raw slits opening up, tender as tentacles. Suddenly he could breathe; but it wasn't breathing, not really.

Staying underwater, he pushed himself right down to the seafloor, stretching out with newly webbed hands to the sand. He could touch every grain, every rock, every strand of eelgrass. This new world felt so right to him. And he was so ridiculously fast! There was no need to return to the surface right now. Not whilst he could swoop into kelp forests, fly around the darkest rock crevices, dance in the tidal currents. Somewhere deep in his mind, he wondered why his legs wouldn't kick as they used to. No, they were better. Way better. He'd never swum so far or so fast underwater before. The view around him was sparklingly acute. Every tiny sprat and floating jellyfish lit up as if glowing with moonshine. If he could see them so clearly, then—he span in circles, checking out his glossy...shiny...tail?

*   *   *

There are two policemen on Scilly, and both agreed wholeheartedly. They saw a single set of footprints in the muddy path by Watermill cove. A measuring tape showed these to be size nine, splayed bare toes clear as daylight where they'd squelched into the soil. Downhill. One way. At the top of the beach lay a muddy pair of chefs' trousers and Steve's tee shirt and jacket.

"It would've been high tide around midnight," they said to Fliss. "No shoes, mind. No doubt about it, though. He must've gone in for a swim. Last thing he ever did."

Fliss raised her hands to her eyes, letting out a cry like a wounded herring gull. "Ohhhh!" she sobbed loudly. "Known Steve a long time, I have. Ohhhh." She turned sideways and crumpled into Jonno.

"Is there a...body?" Jonno asks.

"Well, no." One of the policemen gives him a shrewd look. "Volunteers have been searching the far side of the island all day."

Jonno patted Fliss' back. "I had to be here, for her. Boat's short on fuel, too."

The policeman continued. "That's as may be. Those currents, though...you know them well enough. Helicopters have done a flyby, but..."

"Thank you." Jonno closed the door.

She waited until their footsteps had gone. "Well, bugger him!" she cursed.

"Now, now," Jonno said, hands out, pacifying. "Weren't your fault, were it now?" He wiped away a guilty bead of sweat from his upper lip. "Them currents up at Watermill are evil strong, they are. Can't blame yourself."

"Not that. I don't give a toss about him anymore; you know I don't." Fliss said, slamming one hand out into his broad chest. "How the bleeding heck am I gonna get another pizza chef? So thoughtless, that man. Useless, thoughtless..."

He stared at her. They were still in the honeymoon phase; the loved-up couple who'd snuck into alleyways to be together. Lucked out, he had, sneaking the shapely Fliss from right under Steve's nose. He'd not taken much persuading to invest his savings in her pizzeria, which it sorely needed. That waster hadn't even paid off the ovens. A win-win situation, he'd thought. Fishing made good money on these islands. Reliable money. Fliss could see who was the bigger man. She wasn't stupid. His fishing boat, the Ennis May, was the largest here. That waster Steve only knew how to cook pizza and what was the point in that?

True, he'd not seen Fliss cross before. Perhaps this was grief, manifesting in some way? He hesitated, unsure what to do with her anger.

"Right," he said, "course. Well...best thing I can do is get out there and catch a few fish. Take the edge off us, financially I mean."

"Really?" She pulled a face.

He nodded. "Stuff a sign on the door. No-one expects pizza tonight."

It's midnight, or thereabouts. The Ennis May is chugging around the Eastern Isles. His pots are laid and it's time to ride the flood tide around the north of these uninhabited rocky islands. Throw some nets, aiming for a haul of summer herring. Pollack are abundant here, all glistening silver in the shallows. Bream fetch a pretty penny at the posher end of the market; he can get them onto the Scillonian straight to the fish markets at Newlyn. That'll take the edge off, if he can do it. Oh, Jonno has always been good at spotting where the best fish hide. He's known for watching, waiting, snagging the best. He's got an eye for it, they say in the pub. Fishy by nature, that one. No wonder he took that pretty girl from right under her boyfriend's nose.

Jonno shoves the engine into neutral, uses the hook to rig the nets onto the trawling gear at the stern. He's about to press the button to get the mechanism going, work those nets, see what's there...when something catches his eye. Looking down, under that mysterious full moon, he sees a rounded silver disc. If it were daylight, he'd think that would be a sunfish. They can grow up to a meter in diameter. This isn't quite right though – something about the way it's moving. Where are the fins?

He bends his face over the gunnels, peering closer. This side of the Ennis May is in shadow. The face, for it is a face, stares up through the meniscus of the water. Looks him in the eye. It has long hair, tied back. An unmistakable expression of anger breaks the surface.

Jonno startles. "Steve?"

The sound is thrown from his throat into the salty night air. It's impossible, and yet it happens. The creature that once was Steve launches itself high, broadsiding the steel vessel. The last thing Jonno sees is a muscular tail, shiny scales and fins like flick knives. The last thing Jonno feels is a pair of hands at his throat; grabbing him, dragging him into the sea.

Fish catches fisherman, he thinks, not quickly enough.

Humans can only live without oxygen for a few minutes, and somewhere inside Steve's seaweed brain, he remembers that useful fact. Steve also remembers hating Jonno, wanting him gone. The fisherman's body struggles and then goes limp under dough-strong cold fingers. It floats away on the tide, just below the surface. The engine of the boat is idling in neutral, coughing out fumes of exhaust smoke. The body drifts, nudging up against the hull. Kissing the paintwork.

Was-Steve—Mer-Steve, Fish-Steve, Sea-Steve—thinks again, but the thought processes are slow as iced seawater. He wriggles his tail and shoots away from the boat, sending storms of star-bright phosphorescence in his wake. The anger is gone from his body; deep in his primitive heart is a memory of Watermill Cove and pizzas. Hot ovens, pain. A hot heart, aching for something, or someone. He swims closer into shore, where the men came, this morning. He'd watched them with new fish-lens eyes, in between hunting for sprats, which felt more urgent to this new body with its missing memories.

Tonight, the beach is empty. Somewhere in this back of his mind, he remembers those oven's gaping maws and the crisped crusts of pizzas. In a flash he thinks of her, Fliss. The two-legged one.

He lets out a howled cry and from his new throat it's a cross between rampant seal song and the sound a dolphin makes when dying. There's the strangled high scream of a gull seeking shelter in a storm and the low moan of a blue whale in love. It's beauty and anguish combined.

The sound carries in the darkness, over the hill. It wafts through the open window to where Fliss is sleeping under Jonno's goose down duvet. She stirs, half-asleep, half-entranced. She stands and pulls aside the thick velvet curtains to let the sea air in. The strange sound is louder. It makes her head spin. Must be the wine, she thinks. What to do? She can't help herself: she really fancies a swim. People do funny things when someone dies, she supposes. No point bothering with shoes. She'll just take a good long walk up the hill to Watermill Cove for a quick dip. It will clear her head. As if in a dream, she starts walking.

A Circle of Dragons
by A.J. Pruffrock
Concluded from issue #45, 2023

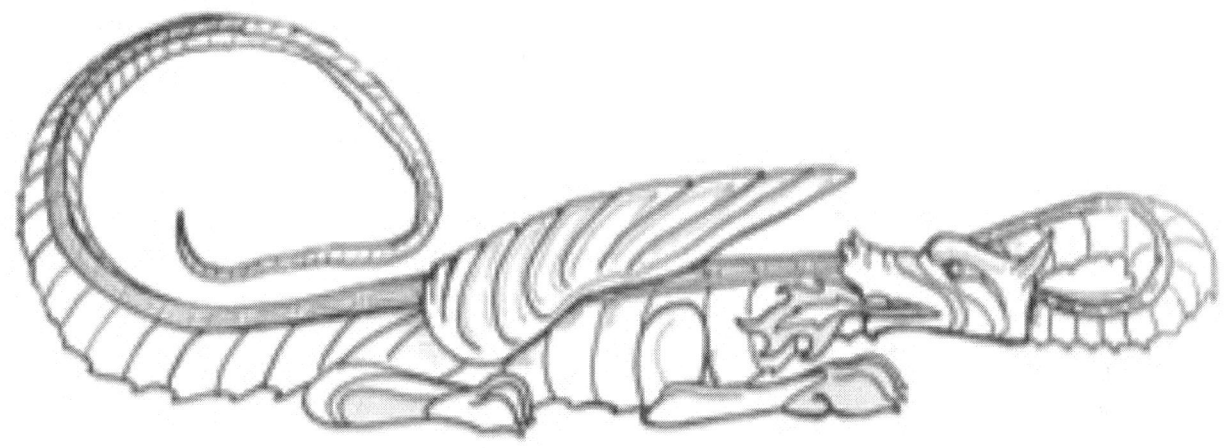

Thuria by Molly Kantz

14. NO STEPMOTHERS ALLOWED

In this chapter, rhymes appear with persistency
This couplet serves to fill the space, for consistency

Just before dawn, Jolene shook Hilda awake. "Get some food for yourself, dearie, and us some more tea. Geraldine wants to hear a story from the beginning. We told her the whole extent of your skills. There may be singing, too!"

Hilda pulled herself up from where she had collapsed before the fire pit and stumbled to the cabin. Upon entering, she washed her face and stepped towards the stove. Her mother had stood here often. What would Mother have done? First, she would make coffee instead of tea. Next, the dragon guests would have to take it black, in regular cups. Mother never would have caved and catered to their dragoniness. They were, after all, visiting a people house.

Hilda decided the guests could very well wait until she tidied up and ate a proper hot breakfast. She thought of assigning the interlopers the chore of gathering firewood. Why not? It would be nothing to them, and it was because of them the woodpile was shrinking. She turned to suggest that very thing, but one determined step across the threshold was as far as the idea ventured. The rising sun illu- mined the hulking mass of reptilian flesh, causing Hilda to shudder. She drew back and collapsed into her mother's place at the family table. "Breathe, Hilda. Pray. Settle your mind into your heart. Find your bearings." Mother's words became her own.

Stepping once again towards the stove, Hilda found that while she had not the courage to insist on help from enemies, she still possessed the wherewithal to help herself. Coffee was set to brew. Ingredients were pulled from cupboards. She would have her fill of cornbread before venturing forth to play hostess once more.

As Hilda puttered, the dragons without prompting minded the fire, using their natural talent to keep flames hot and high. All the lowest limbs of the surrounding trees were broken off and piled nearby. The guests did not seem to notice the wait, and Geraldine prompted them to sing as they busied themselves.

From inside, Hilda did not attempt to follow the lyrics. She was too awash with gratitude that Geraldine had made herself choirmaster, rather than soloist.

Brett only loved the breast and thighs
The neck and head he tossed aside
The skin disdained, the feet long gone
To breasts and thighs his heart belonged

Three-part dragon harmony had a strange charm, but Hilda focused on the comforts close at hand: steaming coffee and melting butter. Her distractedness was for the best, for the words were troublingly insightful into the human condition—

Gail fell in love with shirts and ties
The outline of a chosen man
Enamored by the diamond ring
Gleaming on her hand.

Brett choked last night on boney shard
Gail's honeymoon, an empty thud
Dirty laundry in the yard
Flinging rocks and mud

Hilda waited until the song ended before exiting the cabin with a tray. She served four cups of black brew and sat, offering neither cream nor sugar. The dragons, so focused on handling the delicate stoneware, gave no notice of the contents. They sipped, gulped, stared at their hostess hungrily.

"There is a bit of leftover cornbread ..." Hilda offered.

Geraldine waved her off saying, "I hope I'm in time to sup on something besides leftover stories."

Hilda wiped her hands in her apron, wedged the empty tea tray between the stones she sat upon, and spread her arms. "I welcome requests. What kind of story would you like?"

Geraldine folded her limbs across her breast. "I am as old as these three combined," she declared, nodding towards the underlings, "so no moralizing plots. Give me something to sink my fangs into, like intricate motivations of more than one woman. And no stepmothers. Deliver me from the hoary cliche of stepmothers."

Hilda rubbed her forehead. Neither Jolene nor Wynona was going to speak up for her youth and innocence now. In fact, she wondered if any of the original three were going to speak again at all.

She had survived a single night in the company of dragons and had aged a decade in those dark hours. Perhaps a dark story would be fitting.

ONCE UPON A TIME *there were three royal brothers, Hubert, Dewey, and Lewis. Their parents had passed away and they lived in a great manor house together with their young stepsister Lantana. The brothers loved to hunt and their sister, who hated being left behind, followed them every time they went out tracking in the woods.*

Early one morning, the three princes (with Lantana tagging along, of course) were closing in on a she-wolf creeping her way through the thick underbrush. Hubert drew back his bow, but just before he released the arrow, all three brothers had the shock of their young lives. The wolf spoke. "Do not shoot me! Do not shoot!" she cried, "for I have pups. If you spare me, I will give each of you one of my offspring and all will prove to be faithful friends."

Hubert did not argue. Who would want to shoot a talking wolf? As the group turned and walked away, they found that three little wolves followed, one after each brother.

Near noon, the hunting party approached a lioness sauntering among the brambles. Dewey drew back his bow and just before he released the arrow, all three brothers were surprised to hear the lion speak. "Do not shoot me! Do not shoot!" she cried. "For I have cubs. If you spare me I will give each of you one of my offspring and they will prove to be faithful friends."

Dewey did not argue. Who would want to shoot a talking lion? As they walked away, a little cub followed each of the brothers.

Towards evening, the three brothers drew near to a she-bear ambling her way between saplings. Lewis drew back his bow, but just before he released the arrow, none of the siblings were at all surprised to hear the mama bear speak. "Do not shoot me! Do not shoot!" she cried. "For I have cubs. If you spare me I will give each of you one of my offspring and they will prove to be faithful friends."

Lewis did not argue. Who would want to shoot a talking bear? The group walked away again, now with nine animals padding along behind, three after each brother.

Though it had been the most fascinating hunt of their young lives, Hubert, Dewey, and Lewis were all still itching to fire an arrow. Just before the sun began to set, they came to a clearing in the wood. Three birch trees grew at the juncture of three roads. Three brothers, three trees, three roads, and three of each kind of animal, seemed to them an ominous omen, full of meaning.

"Each of you shoot an arrow into a tree!" exclaimed Lantana, "and I shall read the signs."

Hubert, Dewey, and Lewis shrugged at the odd excitement of their sister as each one shot a single arrow into a birch tree.

80

While the arrows, stuck fast, were still reverberating, Lantana began to walk in a cloverleaf pattern round the trunks. She called for the animals to follow in her train, but none would leave the side of its new master. She pretended indifference and began to sing—

> **Arrows piercing birch wood deep**
> **Wait and watch, each wound will weep**
> **Blood from bark means archer's dead**
> **Milk means nothing yet to dread**

"Goodness, Lantana," said Dewey. "Must you always be so dark and disturbed?"

"I wasn't finished," said Lantana.

"At least sing in a major key," chided Lewis.

"Everybody dies," said Lantana. "The wolf, the lion, and the bear all know it. Why should we lie to ourselves? Anyway, if you had let me continue, you would have heard the next verse which says you all must pick a path—a separate path."

"Go ahead and sing the blasted thing," said Hubert. He was ready to move on, for the sun was getting low.

> **Bid goodbye and part your ways**
> **Come again in forty days**
> **How, in his quest, each one fares**
> **Will tell which man is Father's heir**

Hubert, Dewey, and Lewis conferred. They saw the wisdom of their sister's words. They knew there was a kingdom to rule, yet each one felt the other two more able. Something had to decide the kingship—staring at their accompanying beasts, there was no denying a change was brewing. Three little-traveled roads converging in the woods, three talking animals; these were undeniable harbingers that not even Lewis, the least mystical of the three, could deny.

Lantana, who was used to being left out of conferences and decisions, was surprised when her brothers turned and asked, "Sister, with which one of us do you wish to travel? Choose and tell the others goodbye, for in this wide, wild world, we may never see each other again."

Lantana had already chosen. "I will go with Hubert."

The brothers embraced and separated. They each set out upon a different road, followed by their beasts.

15. HUBERT TAKES THE CASTLE
I'm scented by a great grey wolf
Who watches me throughout the night
This news would cause me great alarm
Except a lion's at my side
The lion too might swallow me
While I sleep sound and unaware
But be assured I rest at ease
Protected by my bear

Hilda paused, wondering from what quarter commentary might come, yet knowing that now there was only one real source of feedback. Geraldine lip-curled below her right nostril and Hilda, though now familiar with dragon facial contortions, could not tell if it was a smile or a sneer.

The elder dragon spoke. "So far, so good. Lantana has spunk ... refuses to be left behind. There might be a lesson for you in that, little human, eh? Must be hard to be left alone in the cabin with the menfolk gone." Hilda did not answer, but stared back unblinking.

Geraldine continued, "The brothers have, to a large degree, dominated their sister's choices. But that era is ending. I am intrigued. You may continue, but enough with the talking animals."

"Yes, Ma'am," answered Hilda, glad the voices of the lion, the wolf, and the bear were no longer crucial to the plot. Placing the empty coffee cups near the tray, she pressed on.

Lantana and Hubert traveled a day and a half along their chosen road. At night they slept soundly, curled in the arms of the bear and the lion while the wolf kept watch. At noon on the second day, they came to a wide glade in the center of which stood a gleaming castle. Hubert bade his animals and sister stay tucked within the woods while he approached and knocked.

The door opened, but instead of being invited in, four rough fellows came out and began to beat Hubert and strip him of his belongings. The attack came without warning. Hubert had no chance to pull his knife or cry out before he found himself face down in the dirt.

The ruffians paused to let him come to his feet, and laughed when he lifted his fists. But Hubert had no need to strike, for out from the woods came his beasts. Each animal, in a flash, had a man by the throat. Hubert took the fourth, dragged him inside, and threw him down into the root cellar with such force that the man lay as one dead.

When Hubert exited the castle, there was neither wounded man nor protective animal in sight. He called for Lantana to emerge from the woods. When he asked for a report of what she had witnessed, she said she had seen nothing, having buried her face in her hands when the violence began.

Lantana took Hubert's arm and they entered the castle together as the sun was beginning to set. There were many large rooms and a fine kitchen, but the place was ill-used and in need of much straightening and scrubbing.

"Brigands are horrible housekeepers," muttered Hubert, "but we will make a go of it. It seems at least all the windows are intact and the doors swing free."

The next morning, Hubert listed out for Lantana the work to be done. He told her that while she cleaned and swept and inventoried the remaining provisions, he would go out to hunt. Perhaps he could find what had happened to his beasts.

"Shall I send the bear back to you if I find him, sister?" he asked. "Though I don't think the man in the cellar will give you trouble since he is most likely dead."

Lantana spit out the bread she had been chewing in a sudden guffaw. Her brother smiled and added, "In any case, he is securely locked in. I'll decide what to do with him tomorrow."

"*Don't bother about the bear, brother,*" *Lantana replied.* "*If you send him, he will not stay. The animals belong to and obey you. Me, they simply tolerate.*"

Hubert shrugged and said, "*You have a great deal to tackle. I hope you can manage without me, but it will be winter soon and I need to replenish what is left of the stores.*"

"*Go ... go,*" *said Lantana.* "*I am not a little girl.*"

LANTANA WANDERED *all through the castle rooms noting unlit chimneys, broken bottles, filthy tapestries, and several ornamental settings with missing gems. I wonder, she thought to herself, where brigands hide jewels. I'll bet they bury them. So down Lantana went, her pace quickening, straight to the cellar door. Herbert had left the keys hanging in the kitchen and these she grabbed along with a large copper scoop to use for digging. If the jewels are not in the cellar, she mused, then I'll ladle up the whole garden.*

Lantana opened the cellar door and stepped over the body of the fourth bandit. Lighting a lamp, she peered down the long and dusty corridor before trodding forward, poking and prodding the musty interior. Though she found several bottles of well-aged wine, Lantana did not see a single jewel nor any sign of freshly dug hiding places.

On her way out, she was pleased to find an iron spade. Dropping the copper ladle in excitement, she decided after lunch she would upend the garden. She was so focused on her plans she did not notice there was no body to step over as she exited. Spade and keys in hand, she turned and relocked the cellar door.

Lantana hummed to herself as she wandered towards the pantry. She hoped there was more day-old bread in one of the cupboards. For though she knew how to cook and had been taught how to clean, she had no intention of doing either. When she arrived in the kitchen, she dropped the spade in shock. There before her was a table set with fine china, wine, grapes, and cheese. And, turning from the stove with spoon in hand was the brigand. Rugged manliness was not diminished by the donning of a well-starched apron, any more than rough-cut winsomeness could be hidden by his one black eye.

"*Madam, I am Morris,*" *said the stranger bowing low.* "*I had hoped to cook for your brother as well, to make up for my earlier bad manners. But to be honest, it is nice to speak to you alone.*"

Lantana said nothing and stepped towards the table.

16. DEWEY BY THE SEA
A dragon a dragon,
I swear I saw a dragon!
Three-headed monster,
quite the beast,
Three minds made up
on me to feast.

Dewey, the second eldest prince, set out on his adventure alone. He traveled a day and a half along his chosen road, sleeping soundly curled in the arms of the wolf, while the bear and lion kept watch.

"*But ... but what about Lantana and Morris!*" *cried out Jolene like one pained.* "*Why did you leave that thread of the story?! I don't care about Dewey!*" *Jolene stamped her back feet in frustration.*

Geraldine spat in the fire and glared. Jolene looked up and whimpered.

"Can you say 'cliffhanger,' Jolene?" Geraldine sneered with edged sarcasm.

"Cliffhanger."

"And," continued the dragon matriarch, "Since I know you cannot define it, perhaps your sister will for you."

Loretta sat up very straight, pressing her fist to her forehead, but no words came.

"Wynona, my pet?" oozed Geraldine, "Would you like to save your classmates once more?"

"Cliffhanger, noun," said Wynona, "a melodramatic or adventure story in which each section ends in high suspense in order to keep a listener's interest. Example in human lore: 'The knight hung on the edge of the cliff as the dragon circled above.' Cliffhanger."

"Who cares about knights?" pouted Jolene.

"Humans do," answered Geraldine, "and unless you wish to be dinner, I expect not another word from your wanna-happy-ending snout."

Jolene nodded. Her shoulders sank, her lower lip jutted out.

"Would you like me to continue?" asked Hilda.

Geraldine bowed. "Pardon Jolene's youth. She will not speak again, and if she does, she will not speak *ever* again."

* * *

At noon the second day, Dewey came to an inn. Leaving his companions in the woods, he entered and spent a coin on food and drink.

Everyone in the inn seemed distressed, so Dewey inquired of those who dined nearby what was the matter. They grunted but told him nothing. After eating, Dewey put his question to the proprietor.

"Ah," replied the innkeeper, "today our lord's daughter is to die, handed over as tribute to a dreadful three-headed dragon."

Dewey looked aghast.

"Don't judge us, son," said the bartender. "The dragon will burn down the town if he is not given his due, and the lord of the manor has grown old. Besides, this is his fifth daughter, who he had hoped would be the first of sons."

84

Dewey thought the death of a beautiful maiden, even fifth-born, was a waste. Knowing himself to be strong, young, and able, he inquired where the exchange with the dragon was to take place. (He was careful to keep his indignation in check.) The half-drunk patrons all pointed in the same direction and answered in chorus, "At the shore, by the sea ..."

As Dewey departed, he heard them continue a drinking song prompted by his request for directions—

At the shore
By the sea
By the beautiful sea
Dragon takes
In the waves
My lady from me

"I will save her," Dewey muttered, "or die trying." And he set out to the seashore, followed by his three beasts.

As Prince Dewey went towards the sea, a great company of people were traveling the same path in the opposite direction. Seeing his bear, wolf, and lion, they gave him wide berth, but Dewey could see on their faces a great sadness. He learned from snatches of their conversations that this was the crowd that had accompanied the princess to her doom.

When Dewey arrived at the shore, he saw a lone maiden bound tight, doing her best to look brave. He also saw, out in the waves a long way off, movement skimming along the tops of the foaming breakers. Across the waters was coming a terrible dragon with three long necks. A grotesque head sat upon each.

The prince, unflinching, took counsel with his beasts.

Bear, wolf, and lion lined up between the damsel and the shoreline, facing the waves. Each dragon neck stretched towards a waiting foe as the gap closed. It would be a great battle—three against three. The damsel, now overwhelmed, fainted dead away. If the dragon won, she was bride to a monster. If he lost, she would be devoured by one of the creatures of the forest. She had not the energy or wherewithal to notice Dewey.

The dragon took no notice of Dewey either, and this suited the prince well. Dewey crouched low and drew his bow, planting one foot in the waves and taking aim perpendicular to the shoreline. The dragon, furious that three beasts stood between himself and the rights due him, paid no mind to his flank. Three necks jutted forward in a triple-synchronized lunge, aiming to plunge teeth into the necks of waiting bear, wolf, and lion. Just as the three heads aligned, an arrow flew. Sharp tip and straight shaft wove through the first head's eye sockets, pierced the second mouth's tongue, and lodged the entirety of the projectile into the ear canal of the third cranium. Searing pain, blindness, dumbness, and deafness followed. Bear, wolf, and lion rushed forward and tore the dragon's body into a thousand pieces.

Hilda wanted no commentary but was sure, at this juncture, it would come. A moment's hesitation was met with silence. She breathed but once, and resumed.

* * *

WHILE THREE BEASTS supped on dragon, Prince Dewey inspected the unconscious damsel. He could tell from the crest on her handkerchief and signet ring that she was from the royal line of Lagobel. It was to that land she needed to return.

She was lovely to behold but not slight in form. Prince Dewey did not know how far he could carry her, and did not think it prudent to harness any of his creatures to pull a stretcher. Besides, it seemed each of them had taken a portion of the carcass to the forest to eat in private. They were nowhere in sight.

Great was Dewey's relief to see a late-coming coach roll up, tardy for the earlier festivities that bid Her Highness adieu. Dewey approached the coachman, explaining all that had transpired, keeping to himself the coordinated effort between man and beasts.

"Climb into the carriage with the damsel," offered the coachman. "I will pass near her father's palace before I cross back over the mountains. Perhaps she will awaken in your arms."

Dewey was relieved, and pulled the sleeping maiden in upon the velvet cushions awaiting them. He sighed at his good fortune and hoped the rescued lady would regain her wits before they had traveled far.

But the coach was not traveling towards Lagobel. It belonged to the damsel's enemies. Hours later, Dewey found himself, bound and gagged, tumbling down the face of a ravine.

17. LEWIS BY THE FIRE

What happens next?
What happens next?
You leave your audience perplexed
How should I know?
How should I know?
The tale is woven as I go!

Prince Lewis took the third path, followed by his faithful beasts.

Geraldine mouthed "cliffhanger," and the other three copied her silent enunciation. Jolene, in particular, was careful that she make not a sound.

Darkness came on, and Lewis curled up in the arms of the lion, as the bear and wolf kept watch. The next morning, halfway to noon, the path came to a dead end. Not wanting to turn back and wander in the same direction as his brothers, Lewis pressed forward as best he could through the underbrush. Hour after hour he fought his way through the brambles, growing more bewildered as the day wore on. The beasts followed doggedly at his disoriented steps as he forged a path into the looming darkness. Then his heart was infused with hope, for the light of a fire leapt up from the shadows ahead.

As Lewis drew near the light, he spied an old woman raking sticks and dried leaves together and burning them in an oblong glade. The prince was weary, darkness was seeping in, so he called out for permission to spend the night beside the old woman's fire.

"Of course you may, young prince," she answered, "but I am afraid of your beasts."

Lewis turned to see. The bear, the lion, and the wolf stood in the shadow cast behind him, and all looked fierce. "They are quite tame. Come see, mother." He bade his lion, and wolf, and bear to lay down and roll over, bellies up. Reluctantly, they obeyed.

The old woman crept up and hid behind Lewis, peeking round him to see that the animals were subdued. With a sudden leap forward she pulled forth a rod and struck each of them. One after the other—lion, and wolf, and bear—they turned to stone.

Prince Lewis stood in shock. Then the old woman, with a gleeful cackle, brought her rod down upon him as well.

Hilda paused. Wynona and Loretta mouthed "cliffhanger." Jolene yipped with shrill excitement, "Back to Morris and Lantana! What happens!? What happens!?"

Geraldine stood up and crossed over to Jolene. Taking her head into her hands, she unceremoniously snapped her neck. Jolene slumped backward and Geraldine returned to her seat before the fire.

"Shall I continue?" said Hilda in a shocked and barely audible voice. The words came only by habit.

"No!" ordered Geraldine. "I've heard enough: three species, three brothers, three women. Trope. Trope. Trope. First, the stepsister must attach herself to a man, a good-brother then a rogue. Classic pretty young female chooses bad boy. Overdone. The second female spends her time unconscious, a helpless victim tied to the stake until plopped down to loll about on velvet carriage cushions. The third female is an old witchy woman in the woods. Nothing new to see here."

Wynona and Loretta sat, mouths open.

Hilda stared at the lifeless Jolene. Would her carcass be dinner for her monstrous companions, or did dragons ever speak in hyperbole?

Loretta raised a hand.

"You may speak, Loretta.

"So no more story ... we're stuck not knowing?"

"Yes. Knowing is useless unless you are learning," growled Geraldine. Loretta, glancing sideways at her very still sister, decided she had no more questions.

"Wynona," Geraldine called out, "Please wrap up the plot for Loretta."

"Well, from the human stories I have heard before," said Wynona with no little arrogance, "I would guess that Morris seduces Lantana and she likes it until she doesn't. Next, Dewey's beasts will help him rescue both his brothers, and he will marry the unconscious princess. I'll bet he has her handkerchief tucked away somewhere as proof of his valor."

Geraldine nodded in half-hidden pride. At least one of her students was progressing.

Loretta blurted, "But ..." then stifled her own mouth.

"Go ahead, Loretta. I don't feel up to killing twice in one day. Jolene will provide plenty for all."

"But," Loretta said, "Dewey is middle-born. Middle-borns never get to marry the princess. I ... I thought that was a rule."

"Good eye! Good ear! Good nose for human plots!" congratulated Geraldine, "but think ... why, in this tale, is there an exception?"

Loretta drummed her forehead with her claws.

"How about you tell us, Hilda?" said Geraldine, swinging round.

"Because he killed the dragon," replied Hilda without hesitation. She saw no harm in stating the obvious and no use in playing dumb.

"Exactly!" puffed the matriarch. "Take this lesson, ladies— a man could be covered in pimples, balding, a fool, produce constant flatulence, and own no more than a belt round his naked waist. But if he kills the dragon in these pathetic people tales, a beautiful, rich, high-achieving, talented, brilliant princess will take him to her bed to produce brat after brat with him."

Wynona and Loretta sat silent.

"Do you know why?" asked Geraldine.

Wynona and Loretta shook their heads.

"Do *you* know why, human? Could you provide some values clarification?"

Hilda shook her head.

"Because," crowed Geraldine, "we dragons are wrapped round the human brain stem. Never forget this, my pupils, and I guarantee you will never become imbedded in one of humanity's over-wrought, over-hyped, over-told tales. We are the basis of all human fears."

18. SPACE TO BREATHE

Dragons in the rafters
Dragons on the floors
Dragons round my campfire
Just outside my door!

Dragon soot on windows
Useless are my locks
Dragon drool and drivel
Splattered on my frock

Geraldine excused Hilda to the cabin while the dragons dined. "It's for your own good," she said. "Don't want to traumatize you any more than we already have." Hilda could hear the crunching and slurping even when pressed against the back interior wall.

When would the men come back? She wondered. Worn down, no longer able to stoke up courage, Hilda felt creeping despair under Geraldine's watchful eyes and critical ears. Should she feel better that now there were only three guests? No comfort came. And there was something tragic about the loss of Jolene, though Hilda had not forgotten her flaming eyes and tightening grip. A ring of bruises on each of Hilda's upper arms testified to the terrible confrontation.

Knowing she had space to breathe until evening, when the next round of entertainment was slotted, Hilda slipped out a back window with a basket for berry picking. She would not be looked for again until the sun began to set. After eating, the dragons would sleep.

Hilda felt her feet wander further and further. Down she went to her old childhood haunt near the streambed. The flow and laugh of the running water calmed her trembling heart and filled her ears with clean pleasantness. If the weather had been warmer, she would have stripped off her dress (spattered with dragon tea and coffee and dribbled with dragon drool and sweat) and plunged in. Even her hair smelled like dragon, and she wanted to wash it away along with every evil she had lately been forced to reckon with.

There was no use running. No one outran dragons. They had to lose interest and this pack was still spellbound. Where was the border between telling a tale too well and telling it too poorly? How did one spin a yarn aptly enough to be valuable alive, but not so mesmerizingly that the audience asked for another, and another, and yet another? She had fulfilled the storytelling task at the highest caliber, and was paying the price for her excellence.

Hilda stared at her tired face in the shallow current. She felt hungry now, but her basket was empty. Another reflection came up, peering over her shoulder. It was Oran's.

Up Hilda leapt with a cry. Older brother had come home; he would know what to do. She splashed across the stream and was at once in his arms.

"It is nice that you come out and greet me, sister," laughed Oran, "but I was rather hoping you would be at the stove stirring something hot. I am famished."

"It is providence you did not get so far, brother," replied Hilda, "for we have guests."
Something in her tone told Oran, and then there was her smell.
"Dragons in the cabin?"

"Well, just outside it ..."

"How many?" Oran asked.

"Do I count the dead?"

Oran raised an eyebrow.

"Three ... very much alive, feeding on one." The siblings sat on the shore together as Hilda continued, "Two Rekikis and one Sarkani—an adolescent, thank God— showed up two days ago. A Zendino joined them in the middle of last night. I am worn out."

Oran gazed at his little sister with a look she had not seen before. Hilda filled her lungs and let out a deep breath, "You smell of dragon too, brother."

"I have been with father, crossing wits with a single Zendino," answered Oran. "You have, in the meantime, been discoursing with three, a Sarkani among them. How in the world have you managed?"

"I served them tea and coffee and told them stories."

"Tea and stories ..." Hilda continued, "And you and Father have been trapped by a Zendino ... your tardiness makes sense now, but Oran, I could use a spotter. You weave fantastic tales ... I feel ready to collapse. It's not just entertainment. I'm the subject of an experiment or an observed animal. One mistake, and I will become an hors d'oeuvre."

"*That* is an accurate assessment, sister, and until they are satisfied, there is not much I can do. A man might tell half a story before he is eaten. How many tales have you made it through?"

"Three ... and a half."

Oran gave a low whistle. "No wonder you're exhausted."

Hilda nodded and sighed. She shuddered realizing three and a half was also the current head count in front of the cabin.

Oran took his sister into his arms. "Hilda, you've done amazingly and you are stronger than either of us thought. I would have been dead before I reached a single plot twist." Hilda squeezed him back and begged, "Can't you at least stay in the shadows, unseen?"

"Perhaps for a bit," Oran said, "but I will be wanted back. Father and I and our one dragon have a kind of short-term truce. The great Zendino says she will return to the lake in the morning with an answer to Father's riddle. I've just come to recuperate for a spell, and grab provisions and ale. Father has not taken well to drinking lake water."

"How long do these trials, these negotiations, go on?" said Hilda, not expecting an answer.

"Ours will end by tomorrow," replied Oran, "for Geraldine has given us her word. If she cannot answer the riddle before tomorrow's sunset, she will never show her face in Lagobel again."

"Her name is Geraldine?"

"Yes."

"That's *my* Zendino. The one eating a Rekiki right now in front of the cabin."

Oran paused and thought as this piece of fascinating information was sorted and put in its place.

"She's heard your stories," he said at last. "Does she know your station?"

"I am a youngling, a simple country maiden to my guests.

They order me about, and I do not protest. They have no interest in personal history. They crave sagas, lore, stories of 'the peoples.'"

"Research ... she's doing research," Oran mused aloud. "She supposes the more she knows of humans, the better her chances of answering Father's riddle. How blessed we are that she has not guessed that she has Kenterick kin in her clutches."

"Should you tell me the riddle, so I won't betray you and father through ignorance?" asked Hilda.

Oran thought for some time, paced several strides back and forth along the bank, then answered, "No. Knowing would change your tone, your posture, your simplicity."

"But what if I give something away? What if she guesses my connections?"

Oran pulled at his beard. "Do you know "The Ring and the Drow-Maiden?"

Hilda nodded.

"Tell your guests that one. It will infuriate Geraldine but it will bring her no closer."

"An infuriated Zendino on my hands," said Hilda. "Thanks."

"Hopefully," quipped Oran, "it doesn't also piss off the Sarkani."

***Mushroom Glass,* by Phillip Fitzsimmons**

19. THE RING AND THE DROW-MAIDEN

Boris the dwarf spoke slowly to Gleb
Most of his words went over Gleb's head

That evening, Hilda sat silent. The dragons waited. Hilda crossed her arms. Loretta twiddled her thumbs. Wynona did her best to mirror all the movements and gestures of Geraldine.

"What is it, youngling?" said Geraldine. "One more is not much to ask. Your break went long and our bellies are full. There is no danger of being eaten at present."

Hilda shook her head. "Not another 'once upon a time' until I have some assurances."

"Well, well ... finding your own mind and voice, are you?"

Geraldine turned towards Wynona. "This could get very educative. Pay close attention. What kind of assurances, human, do you wish for?"

Hilda did not hesitate. "One—when I say, 'The End,' it is not just the end of another story but the end of our acquaintance. You three leave and I stay, just as I am, with my home intact. Two—take off the prohibition on either talking animals or stories with stepmothers. It leaves my options unbearably narrow."

"And if we refuse?"

"No story. I figure you'll eat me either way ... unless you promise." Hilda now twiddled her own thumbs in feigned casualness. "I have heard dragons are wary of breaking their word."

"Which is why we rarely give it," said Geraldine.

"Well, give me your word," shot back Hilda, "or shove me down your gullet now to join Jolene."

Geraldine stroked her beard, "You, little one, so young, barely from your egg ... already fighting and conniving. You could be one of us."

"I am human, ma'am, one of the peoples," said Hilda with ferocity. "We do not do as dragons do."

"Really ... ?" said Geraldine, picking up a stray bone to clean her teeth. "Are you sure?"

Hilda did not flinch. "Did you hear my conditions? Do you give your word?"

"Let me see. One—we must leave at 'The End,' with your property, life, and limbs intact. If you get to the end, then yes, you have my word. And two—talking animals or stepmothers ... which one ... hmm. You may have the animals."

"Your word."

"I, Geraldine of the Greater Zendino, give you my word." Hilda rose, threw a log in the fire, and began.

The Sarkani, the great dragons of the north, are breathtaking to behold. They lay waste to whole tracts of country, devouring both men and beasts. Those who see them and survive say they have a body like an ox—but bigger times five—and hind legs like a bullfrog, not slimy but sinewy and spring-loaded, able to catapult the beast forward ten times its body length. The forearms, by comparison, are quite short. A third set of long appendages protrude just inside Sarkani shoulder blades, forming bat-like wings. The mighty tail grows with the dragon, always remaining twice as long as the beast to which it belongs.

Sarkani skin is an intricate network of interlocking scales, harder than stone. Its two great eyes pierce daylight and shine like searchlights by night. Anyone who looks into those great shining orbs becomes bewitched, rushing of his own accord into the monster's jaws.

Wynona stood up, unfurled her wings, and jutted out her long snout towards the sky. She was, even in her youth, a sight to behold. She held her pose for a long ten seconds, then folded her pinions, laced her clawed fingers, and sat to listen once more.

When a Sarkani appeared in the central kingdom of Endelion, ten years before the great earthquake, all animosity between jurisdictions disappeared. Neighboring kings forgot petty rivalries and formed cooperatives. Rulers pooled resources to offer rich incentives. Multiple king's daughters were set out as possible brides for any man able to destroy the monster, whether by force, trickery, or enchantment. One king who shall go unnamed offered two daughters, willing to wed both to one man.

Sarkani dragons, it was rumored, might be overcome by riddles, magic rings, or the promise of gold. Gleb of Glenbrook had none of these things. But the idea of a woodsman marrying a princess fascinated him. One of the king's daughters had caught his fancy. (One wife would be plenty for him--Gleb knew just enough to shudder at the idea of two.)

Daydreams of heroic deeds and young love were transformed to practical necessity when Gleb realized the beautiful woodland in which he lived was in danger. The dreaded beast was moving ever nearer. When a Sarkani takes possession, it moves on only after it scorches the earth down to bedrock, burning away not just trees and underbrush but the very topsoil. Gleb thought that possibly he might be at the beginning stages of love for a certain princess, but he knew he loved the trees. And, if the forest was turned to barren wilderness, he could not earn his bread. He was very certain of his need to eat.

* * *

A DWARF NAMED Boris lived at the heart of Glenbrook Forest.

At the word "dwarf" all three dragons, in chorus, humphed and rolled their eyes.

Boris had made a hand-carved home within the third-largest tree. He had little interest in princesses and even less in dragons. He had no need to earn his bread since he squirreled away nuts for sustenance, just enough and no more to keep his small body alive. But Boris loved the trees as much as Gleb. In this, they understood one another.

The dwarf was not unaware of the dragon's nearness, so he mentioned to the woodsman in passing that one might— perhaps—maybe discover the secret to killing a Sarkani dragon if one could gain the signet ring once possessed by the famed King Glockenspiel. Glockenspiel's ring was perhaps—maybe—possibly engraved with an inscription with instructions on how a brave man might—maybe—vanquish the encroaching nemesis. Also, in a tiny script etched with a fairy needle, along the shining rim of the golden ring, a second inscription instructed how a courageous warrior might—perhaps—maybe survive.

Gleb thanked Boris, surprised not only that the tree-dwelling dwarf spoke a well-educated King's English, but that they shared the same burning concern. Hoping to continue the conversation, Gleb ventured a question, "Where do you think the ring is now?"

"I can only suggest a direction," answered Boris. "East. All wisdom worth knowing these days comes from the East."

"Could you elaborate a bit further?" said Gleb, keeping his tone polite but firm. He had heard dwarfs would not converse with those who did not demand respect.

Boris sighed and said (more to himself than to Gleb), "There's nothing for it but to teach him bird."

"Bird?" said Gleb. "You want to give me a bird?"

"Their language," said Boris, now wishing he had not begun the conversation in the first place. "The birds of the air will guide you, if you learn to understand their chatter."

"I did not make good marks in school," said Gleb, now wishing he had not asked any further questions. "Languages, even my own native tongue, get all twisted when I make an effort to pin them down. I have often daydreamed," he continued, sighing (more to himself than to Boris), "of a rune, or a spell, or a potion that puts the knowledge inside me all at once."

"There is a way," muttered Boris. He wondered now if he would have a single trade secret left at the end of the interchange. He bade Gleb sit as he mixed a powerful brew of nine herbs gathered alone by moonlight. Of this he gave Gleb nine spoonfuls and ordered him to return for a second and third dose over the next three days.

After the last dosage, Gleb heard not another word from Boris except, "Go east, listen to the birds, and if you ever find Glockenspiel's ring come back to me. I may be able, by then, to perhaps—maybe—explain the inscription to you."

"Both inscriptions," said Gleb, but Boris made no answer.

* * *

THE FIRST WEEK of Gleb's travel was tedious. He felt a meaningless aimlessness set in, as though very little, if any, progress were being made. He grew tired, and hot, and bored with walking.

The second week of Gleb's travel was monotonous. He felt the meaningless aimlessness set in to his bones, like no progress at all was being made. He grew more tired, and hot, and bored with walking.

The third week of Gleb's travel felt counter-productive. He was overwhelmed by meaningless aimlessness, a sense of regression and uprooted purposelessness. He was tired, and hot, and bored with walking.

At the beginning of the fourth week, Gleb, hot and tired and bored, sat down under a tree in a strange forest to eat his supper. After a few bites of dried bread, he noticed that two rose-breasted yellow-plumed silverbeaks sat above him. The birds looked down upon the human quizzically. One said to the other, "That is a wandering fool—a stultus errans.*"*

Geraldine grunted but held her tongue. Hilda pretended not to notice.

"I believe you are right in your classification, my dear," said her mate. "He is far from his conclave and migrating erratically. I wonder if he, having come so far, will find what he is looking for."

The bird-wife was quick to answer, "He will have to seek help from the drow-maid. If she has not got what he wants herself, she will know well enough who has it."

"But where is he to find the drow-maiden?" said her husband. "He might as well try to catch the wind."

"Once a month she comes to a nearby spring to wash her face under the light of the full moon."

"That is in three days' time," mused the husband-bird. "I never understood her ritualistic washing, and why once a month?"

"As to the interval," said the wife-bird, "I have not the energy to explain, but as for why she washes, she does so to never grow old. Coming to the spring keeps her wrinkle-free and in the bloom of her youth."

"We should fly to the spring," said the husband-bird, winking. "Perhaps the stultus errans *will follow."*

"Yes! Yes!" chirped his wife and away they flew.

Gleb somehow tracked the rose-breasted yellow-plumed silverbeaks, though he often lost sight of them. The birds, for their part, enjoyed the novelty of being followed, but forgot more than once that the wandering fool had no wings to carry him along. They never noticed that Gleb's heart beat with anxiety lest he should lose sight of his guides.

At last, the birds reached a clearing in the forest and settled to roost at the top of a high tree. A clear spring bubbled in the middle of the green space below. Gleb sat down at the foot of the birds' chosen perch to watch and listen. The silverbeaks went on and on, chattering, not caring whether or not they were understood.

"When the drow-maiden comes to the spring, do you think, husband, that she will be dissuaded from bathing by the wandering fool? She is quite secretive you know."

"Nothing escapes her notice," said her spouse. "It will be a fascinating interaction. But I think the main question is whether or not the youth has the sense to not let himself get caught in her coils."

"Wait and see, wait and see," came the wifely answer.

* * *

THE MOON WAS SHINING *down upon the forest when Gleb heard a slight rustling sound.*

From the west side of the clearing, out of the forest came a maiden gliding over the grass. Her feet seemed scarcely to touch the ground.

Gleb could not turn away his eyes. He had never in his life seen a woman so beautiful. None of the princesses from the kingly co-op could compare.

The drow-maiden drifted straight to the spring where she stood looking up to the full moon. She knelt down and bathed her face nine times, stood, and faced skyward again. She walked nine times round the spring and as she went, she sang—

> **Full-faced moon with light unshaded,**
> **Let my beauty ne'er be faded.**
> **Aged wrinkles now forbid!**
> **Though the moon is waning nightly,**
> **May my youth bloom always brightly,**
> **Gnarling greying ever hid.**

The maiden dried her face with her long hair, and was about to go back under the shelter of the trees when her eye caught sight of the youth watching slack-jawed. She crossed the green lawn towards him with ever quickening pace. Gleb stood up, waiting.

Her voice was stern and cutting. "You presumed to watch my secrets in the moonlight! Who are you? How have you come to this place?"

Gleb, somehow finding his voice, said, "Forgive me, beautiful maiden, for offending you. I chanced to come here after a long wandering and was resting under the tree. When you came, I did not know what to do, so I stayed where I was. I did not think that my watching would offend you. I see now I was wrong."

Hearing his answer, the tone of the drow-maiden changed. "Come. It is better to rest upon a pillow than upon damp moss. You shall spend the night under my roof."

Gleb was amazed at this turn of events, but hesitated. The birds called from the top of the tree assuring him—

> **Go, go, she calls, she calls**
> **The ring, the ring, go go**
> **but give no blood**
> **no blood, no blood**
> **or she will have your soul.**

20. Dragon Flame

How can I believe you
Unless you show me?
My little darling,
Don't you know me?

The garden of the drow-maiden was magnificent to behold. Beyond the beautiful lawn stood a splendid house, glittering in the moonlight, gilded in gold and silver. When Gleb entered the palace, he found many sumptuous chambers lit by hundreds of tapers burning in golden candlesticks.

At length, the maiden led him to a room where a feast was spread upon ornate silver dishes. His hostess seated herself in a golden chair, and offered a silver one to Gleb. They dined in silence, served by maids dressed in white.

Gleb felt overcome by the beauty of his surroundings, the aliveness of his taste buds, and the softness of their after-dinner conversation. The drow-maiden took his arm and led him though room after room until she herself tucked him into a silken bed under a downy comforter. The last words he heard her say before sinking into euphoric sleep were, "Would you not like to stay here always? I do not age, am very rich, and have no guardian. We can do as we like."

The next morning, while Gleb dressed for breakfast, the maiden herself brought him a tray. She wore a look that expected an answer.

Gleb took her hand with gentle caution saying, "Don't be angry, dear maiden. I do not decide in haste on any important matter. And what could possibly be more important than whether or not I remain with you?"

"But of course!" she breathed in rushed interruption. "Take weeks if you like to know your heart." She pressed Gleb's hand to her chest and added, "I am Gwyllion, my darling. I do not honor many with my true feelings, much less my name."

Gleb nodded and she left him to eat alone with his thoughts.

Gleb did not see Gwyllion again until dinner. He passed his time wandering the halls. The air felt thick with enchantment, but all five of his senses testified to the reality of wall, and rug, and tapestry. Gleb did not know what course of action to take, and was no closer to discerning it when he was summoned to dinner.

*After another silent meal, Gwyllion took Gleb to a secret chamber where a little gold box stood on a silver table. "Here is my greatest treasure," she said, "a precious gold ring which will be yours when ... I mean **if** ... you marry me." She smiled and her eyes shone bright.*

"It is indeed beautiful," admitted Gleb.

"See the small stone in the center, how it glows?" Gwyllion went on. "Tradition says a groom, on his wedding eve, pricks the smallest finger on his left hand and wets the gem with a drop of his own blood. In doing this, the ring brings the wearer to heights of wedded bliss, and the couple's love lasts until death ... sometimes even beyond."

Gleb, determined to guard his soul, hid his feelings. He took the maiden's hand in his and said, "I am overwhelmed by even the thought of such a gift. Tell me more about this magical ring, for I struggle to believe it."

"No one fully understands," Gwyllion said, "because no one can read the secret signs engraved upon it. I'm told it once belonged to King Glockenspiel of Endelion, whoever he was. Still, even without knowledge of the runes, I can work great wonders with it."

"Show me, darling," breathed Gleb.

She said, "If I put the ring upon the little finger of my left hand—I can fly like a bird through the air, wherever I wish to go. If I put the ring upon the fourth finger of my left hand—I am invisible, and can see everything that passes round, though no one can see me. If I put the ring upon the middle finger of my left hand—neither fire nor water nor any sharp weapon can hurt me. If I put the ring upon the thumb of my left hand—that hand becomes so strong that it can break rocks and shatter walls."

Gleb stood dumbfounded as Gwyllion put the ring back into its box.

"My darling," said Gleb with an eyebrow upraised, "I want to believe all that you say, but it sounds like legend, like a bedtime story."

Gwyllion reopened the box.

"Perhaps," she said, "seeing is believing." The ring glittered like the clearest sunbeam as she held it out. The maiden put it on the fourth finger of her left hand, and she disappeared from sight.

"Do not tease me!" called out Gleb. "My heart aches, my love, when I do not see you!"

With that Gwyllion reappeared and smiled. "It is my turn now," Gleb said with a wink. And Gwyllion handed him the ring.

Gleb, without hesitation, put the ring on the little finger of his left hand, and soared into the air like a bird.

Gwyllion saw him fly and cried, "Come back down now, my love. My heart aches when you are not beside me. And now you see I have told you the truth."

Soaring ever higher, Gleb was gone.

* * *

GLEB DID NOT HALT *or even slow until he reached the home of Boris. The dwarf was delighted to find that Gleb's search had been successful. The Sarkani dragon was drawing ever closer and both could smell the smoke.*

Boris at once set to work interpreting the secret signs engraved upon the ring. There was no potion or herb to speed the learning this time, and it took him forty days' hard work to squeeze the meaning from the engraving. Three days more were required to interpret the tiny script, etched with a fairy needle, round the shining rim.

In the end, both dwarf and man knew how to overcome the great Sarkani of the north, but neither was certain Gleb would survive.

Wearing Glockenspiel's ring upon the correct finger at each juncture in battle was crucial. Taking no weapon but the ring was implicit. Boris warned Gleb multiple times over to let no one take it from him by force or by cunning.

Gleb embraced Boris, in spite of his stiffness, and thanked the dwarf for his aid and wisdom. "We will share the rewards together, if honors and treasures there be."

Boris shook his head. "The ring, this short time in my hand, has given me much. I need no other reward. Go and save our forest."

* * *

DURING THE WEEKS spent deciphering the runes, the dragon had moved quite close. It was devouring the land just over the mountains in places where the kingdom of men touched the frontier. Boris chose to sequester himself in his tree and not watch the confrontation. But he could not escape the noise of battle when Gleb and the beast began to brawl.

The dragon met Gleb with jaws wide open, expecting the usual quick surrender of its prey. Gleb trembled with horror but though his blood ran cold, he did not lose his courage. The befuddled beast lunged again and again at a disappearing, then reappearing, then disappearing, then reappearing foe. At times the man seemed to fly. The roaring fire of dragon's breath for the first time missed its target. Or did it? Nothing—man nor beast, hill nor dale, tree nor flower—had ever escaped the heat of the mighty Sarkani. How was it now made ineffective? The ever-shifting battle was dizzying to a dragon used to nothing but spiritless surrender.

Boris, over the mountains, heard a fearful clap of thunder when Gleb lifted the tip of the Sarkani's great tail aloft. Glockenspiel's ring glittered on his left thumb. As Gwyllion had promised, his hand was imbued with the power to break rocks and shatter walls. With this strength, Gleb, left-handed, impaled the monster through the lower jaw. The dragon's own pointed appendage pierced through its hideous mouth. With a second thrust, Gleb forced the spike up and into the great lizard's brain.

The death struggle of the monster lasted three days and three nights. The writhing tail, yanked free at last from its head, beat the ground with such violence that a ten-mile radius trembled as if from an earthquake. When at length the beast lay quiet, Gleb moved forward and removed its head as a trophy. This he took to the circle of kings.

In her peripheral vision, Hilda noted Wynona's eyes glowing like burning coals. Geraldine looked to Hilda and then Wynona, paying as much mind to her Sarkani companion now as to the story. The heightened tension between the two made the fact that Loretta had gone missing almost an afterthought.

The conqueror was received with great adulation. Gleb's chosen princess needed no convincing, and a magnificent wedding was celebrated within a fortnight with fireworks and parades.

GWYLLION, meanwhile, was plotting a hellish revenge. She wondered how Gleb expected to live happily-ever-after in the arms of a beautiful princess as a king's son-in-law. How bitterly she rued the day she had ever trusted him. Her fury was tremendous. She had favored a mortal with her love and he had repaid her with treachery and theft. She had required but a drop of blood upon a gemstone. Having long ago forgone her own soul, Gwyllion had no way to understand why Gleb still valued his.

The dragon lay where Gleb had slain it, and the monstrous body began to rot. The smell emanating from the corpse poisoned the air of multiple kingdoms. Gleb was called upon to solve the problem he had helped create. He decided, once more, to seek the wise advice of Boris.

If Gleb had not been high on young love, he would have been more prudent. He would have walked or ridden with a measure of stealth when traveling back to the forest. Instead, Gleb chose to use the magic ring and fly, and by this Gwyllion found and tracked him. Who, other than the lover that had spurned her, would leap from a turret and glide to a soft landing in the forest? By powers older and darker and swifter than King Glockenspiel's ring, Gwyllion arrived before Gleb at the dwarf's home.

When Gleb knocked, Boris's hand reached out through the window in the trunk of his tree. On its palm Gleb placed Glockenspiel's ring. But the arm of Boris was no longer attached to Boris himself. The drow-maiden had wasted no time.

"Stop," cried Geraldine.

Hilda looked about. Sometime during the story, Wynona had grown. Or had Geraldine shrunk? Hilda could no longer tell which dragon out-fleshed the other.

"How is it ..." said Wynona leaning in, her head above the campfire flames. Tongues of fire now drew back in dread of the greatness of a full-grown Sarkani. "How is it, little girl-human, that the story you weave builds up so nobly the awesomeness of the Sarkani, and then dispatches greatness in less than a page with a flimsy piece of magic jewelry? By what lies do you peoples live, that make your tales build more dread of womanhood than of dragon?"

Geraldine tried to intervene. "The point of the story, Wynona, is that Gwyllion's womanhood was distracting Gleb's manliness from his noble life mission ..."

"Stop!" screamed Wynona. "I am done with your lectures. My people are dishonored. This young human will not tell this tale, or any other, ever again."

"The End," said Hilda flatly. "Thus concludes the tale. The. End."

Both dragons glared.

Hilda stared in return. "Keep. Your. Word."

Both dragons took a step backward.

Wynona looked around. Geraldine unfurled her wings, "I have an appointment to keep. Wynona, come."

Wynona's eyes looked into Hilda's. In that single split second, before shutting fast her lids, the maiden tasted dragon's fire. When Hilda opened her eyes again, she had a splitting headache, but she was alone.

The fire was sputtering out.

The moon was rising high.

From the cabin wafted the smell of raisins steamed in porridge.

Oran was minding the stove.

The River to the Ethereal Valley
by Christopher Collingwood

Manufactured by Amazon.ca
Bolton, ON